# Andrea's Dream

## Enchanted Alaskan Proprietress

Robert Algeri

Author of Alaska Romantic Fiction

PUBLICATION
CONSULTANTS
We Believe In The Power Of Authors

*PO Box 221974 Anchorage, Alaska 99522-1974*
*books@publicationconsultants.com—www.publicationconsultants.com*

ISBN Number: 978-1-59433-949-3
eBook ISBN Number: 978-1-59433-950-9


Library of Congress Catalog Card Number: 2020940620


Copyright 2020 Robert Algeri
—First Edition—

Manufactured in the United States of America

# *Contents*

## Introduction

# *Andrea Mona Altiery*

It's 1996, and I find myself flying back to Alaska for the first time in thirteen years. I get to explore in the Last Frontier for twenty-seven days, alone. I recently had a dream of a gentle, smiling swan of a woman, graceful and elegant. She has been calling my name across the midnight waters. Her name is Andrea Mona Altiery.

When I get into Anchorage, my goal is to locate her if possible. We lost contact back in 1981. I am eager to begin my search. I am going to start by searching all the jewelry stores in the Anchorage downtown and midtown areas, do some shopping like any good tourist should, ask a few questions, and maybe get a few answers along the way.

There comes a point during your flight to Alaska when the lights go down. Most people go to sleep or put their headphones on and disappear into a dream. This can be a reflective moment for anyone who finds themselves staring down into that vast, deep wilderness, with wandering thoughts, alone in their mind. It causes me to reflect for a moment on a quote I had recently read from Homer, in his book *The Iliad*.

In *The Iliad*, Homer says, "We the gods will live, as long as all the humans believe in us, the day the humans no longer believe in us, we the gods will disappear." This is when I realize for the first time in my life that centuries ago Scandinavian gods, Greek gods, and Roman gods were worshipped by hundreds of thousands of people. Today we know them as legends or as characters in popular movies. When we stop believing in lies, all the lies will disappear.

What do you think you will be most remembered for when you move on from this life? Sometimes not knowing the answer may be better than actually knowing.

# Chapter 1

# *Andrea Altiery Arctic Swan*

As I curl up in my seat to relax, my mind drifts off into what becomes an alarming dream. Pool balls clack together loudly in the background, the echo rumbling across the lounge toward me. The bartender is profusely ringing a large tip bell. The bell is hanging off a wooden post next to the bar. Her raucous ringing indicates her evening is going very well for her financially tonight. *It's a lucrative career tending bar in the Last Frontier this evening for the pretty girl dressed in plaid*, says the bell.

I know I have been in this building before; this place is eerily familiar, but I just can't quite place it. I vaguely saw 335 Boniface Parkway on the building as I came in, but I wasn't able to pause long enough to read, so it seems hazy. I am almost certain I've been in this parking lot that sits at the big corner and along the curve that leads out onto the Glenn Highway.

The building itself reminds me of an old Western saloon that's standing alone in a desert oasis. The setting offers vivid glimpses of the Chugach Mountains, rippling across the near horizon. Wolf packs and wolverines roaming blustery valleys, night predators on the prowl as their eyes scan, hot noses working the scent, long slow breaths, inhaling deeply.

I slowly approach the bar, while glancing at sad faces in a crowd—motionless, they peer back. I raise my hand and motion for the bartender. Smiling, she comes my way. She is wearing a purple plaid shirt and has a black scarf tied around her neck. Her name tag says Robin. I introduce myself while ordering a shot of whiskey. Robin smiles and replies, "Sure, will that be it, cowboy?"

I decide to take a chance and ask Robin if she has seen my missing swan. "Robin, I am looking for a graceful woman. She is elegant like a swan." Robin's smile becomes extremely unpleasant. She starts laughing hysterically at me. Frantically she starts waving her hands at me to leave. Startled and frightened, I quickly back up toward the door, smashing into the juke box with a hard jolt. Quickly and unexpectedly, crippling panic washes over me and overtakes my mind. My head is spinning. My crazy, wide eyes are scanning the crowd.

I can hear and feel the lyrics that are pumping through the juke box speakers. The lyrics are screaming out a story about someone who is wanted, dead or alive. Without warning, a stocky, thick-necked man walks over to me and sharply points his finger into my face. He snarls into my face, with his hot, fierce breath, "Bad things are coming for you, pretty boy. You might want to leave this place right now."

I can feel the sound wave of the lyrics as they continue screaming at me from the juke box. The people I meet seem to always go their separate ways. Sulky and gloomy, my back against the wall, I find myself looking at a picture that's hanging on the wall. In the picture there is a blonde girl sitting in a big cocktail glass. The smiling blonde girl is wearing red high heels, red undies, and a red bra. Her cocktail glass is held high, while she is toasting all who enter and exit the bar.

Suddenly I am standing outside in an unlit corner of an empty, windy parking lot. I am looking back toward a brown building with orange lettering on it. I can read a big orange banner that runs along a second floor balcony—it reads Carpentiers Lounge. I look back across the parking lot and can see a lone pickup truck with a camper on it—it's sitting off in the distance, idling. Loud echoing sounds start to wash across the parking lot. I can hear the exhaust making a crackling sound, and it's reverberating into a crescendo as the sound washes back toward me in an acoustic wave.

I see someone step out of the shadows and start walking toward the idling pickup truck. *I think they must be meeting up.* The truck's backup lights come on, allowing me to see it is tilting to the left on its suspension. As the truck starts to slowly back out of its parking space, I recognize that truck, and the crackling sound of the exhaust. As I am watching the person who is approaching the truck, I recognize the walk, the bounce to the step. This is all eerily familiar and becoming unsettling in a primal way, sudden needs and fears fighting for attention in my clouded mind. Is this what I think it is?

I can see it's a woman who is walking toward the idling pickup truck, and she is wearing a pair of brown suede leather boots that are knee high. They have big laces that run the full length up the back of her calves. Her walk is graceful and smooth, with a small bounce to it. Her head is slightly rocking back and forth with each step she takes. It's Andrea Altiery, my missing swan. I begin to jump up and down, frantically waving both hands above my head trying to get her attention. I start screaming and shrieking, my vocal chords straining against the pressure, "ANDREA, DON'T … ANDREA, NO … ANDREA, NO," but Andrea doesn't hear my shouts tonight. Suddenly I panic and feel a wild urge to flee wash over me …

I wake up with a jolt that is being caused by extreme turbulence, as our plane starts dropping down through a small squall over Cook Inlet. I start looking around as myself and all the other passengers get sharply jolted back into our conscious realities. Anthony, the man sitting next to me, doesn't wake up. He keeps snoring. His head is bouncing off my left shoulder to the rhythm of the vibration that is shuddering through the plane. I decide to let him ride it out. Why interrupt his dreams? Dream on, Anthony my friend. Hopefully he will awaken to a bounty of sweet emotions.

Our flight attendants diligently and meticulously go through the preparation for our landing. I can feel the excitement as it begins sweeping through the cabin of our plane. As we touch down on the awaiting runway, our plane is stable and true as it grips the runway's pavement. Suddenly, "SNAP," the sound of the click. I hear two hundred seat belts being unclipped at the same time, opening the way for life's adventures in the great land. Welcome to the Last Frontier.

# Chapter 2

# *Depression Beneath Denali*

I am able to grab my rental car very quickly today because they have a large staff working the counters doing customer service duties. The kids at the counter are enthusiastic and helpful. Everyone is smiling and excited for the upcoming weekend.

It seems like it is always windy when I arrive at the airport in Anchorage, and today is no exception for me. We also have overcast skies with a light rain kicked in for added pleasure, just in time to get my search party started.

I am staying in a familiar location at the Historic Anchorage Hotel on the corner of E.3rd Ave and E St downtown Anchorage. I am enjoying my ride up through Spenard Rd toward the downtown area. As I approach the intersection of Spenard Rd and West Northern Lights Blvd, a group of people wearing backpacks are all walking across the parking lot of the REI store. It looks like twenty to twenty-five people are all going on a backpacking trip.

Momma O's restaurant is coming into view up on my left, and at the same time there it is, the windmill located at Chilkoot Charlie's, with its red, white, and blue light bulbs attached to the length of its legs. I have stood and looked up at this windmill many times in the past, the 26th Ave and Spenard Rd street signs etched in my memory. They have it surrounded by a chain link fence topped with barbed wire, hoping to dissuade would-be trespassers from climbing up it, possibly falling and sustaining severe bodily injury during their quest for local notoriety.

I love the drive along Spenard Rd, especially the stretch that runs north from the intersection, with Fireweed Lane up into the merge with Minnesota Drive and into I St. While I am passing by the big building that houses the Sunrise Bakery, I remember my interview at a bakery over in the downtown area off 9th Ave back in 1981—Hansen's Bakery. The man I met with that day kept calling himself Bob the Owner. I never did encounter him again, that I am aware of.

As I drive into the Westchester Lagoon area, I get my first real feeling of being back in Anchorage, being back home in the shadows of the sleeping lady. The nagging question in my mind is, *Will she remember me?* As I drive across 15th Ave and merge into I St, I begin my last stretch of the drive into the heart of downtown Anchorage. I can see the blue of Sagaya Oriental Grocery approaching up on my left; Marriott red dominates the skyline above and to my right.

I continue my drive along I St until it ends at the intersection with W.3rd Ave. As I am turning left onto W.3rd Ave, I start to pass through an area of nice business buildings. I need to find a parking spot, and there we go—there are several parking spots available up ahead and on my right. Overcome with anticipation, I start to shake while I am attempting to take the keys out of the ignition, my fumbling fingers not quite grabbing when I need them to grab, causing me to get distressed and frustrated.

While I am walking the short distance over to Resolution Park, my mind begins to wander to thoughts of Andrea Altiery. My vivid and complex dreams of her that have led me back to Alaska and to this spot. We walked together in this area a lot, and she revealed her dreams to me down along the waterfront. Andrea always enjoyed looking ahead and planning for her future, which is why I need to go check out 533 W.4th Ave to see if I can find a door that has her name on it.

Now that I find myself standing below the Captain Cook statue once again, it doesn't seem to have the same appeal it had for me thirteen years ago. I was expecting my spirit to soar and sing at the sight of Susitna. Instead I find an eternal heartache that will never cease. There has been no dancing in the land of Denali for my sleeping lady. Her body has found no rest in my absence. Her unsettled spirit is eternally searching as she gazes out upon the frozen ground.

A group of giggling flight attendants from Japanese Airlines, with JAL name tags, interrupt my thoughts. Using hand signals combined with broken English, they ask me to take pictures of them as a group, and then individually. They are bubbling with excitement, which becomes contagious within seconds of my being in their presence. I get handed at least twelve different cameras and then pulled into at least seven group photos with girls I have never met before. Maybe the tides of good fortune have turned for me today; maybe the gods of love are smiling upon me.

As the group of flight attendants turn away from me to leave the park, one of the girls breaks away, and comes running back over to me, smiling. She reaches out and vigorously shakes my hand. I notice all the women are wearing the same uniforms—nice blue blazers, sharp and trim. If you pay attention and look closely enough, each girl has a way of accessorizing that makes each uniform unique—the tilt of their caps, where they place their pins, ribbons or no ribbons, red scarf tucked, or untucked.

It's the women's individual faces that tell me the true story, though. It's a story of love lost, love that hasn't been found yet, and, for some of these women, love that will never be found at all. While the flight attendant girl is looking up at me and vigorously shaking my hand, her dark, chocolate-brown eyes begin to melt my heart, but then I notice she is looking right through me, like I'm not even there.

I coldly turn away from the girl's empty gaze, to look out across Cook Inlet, when I notice the city lights of Anchorage are being turned down for the night. Suddenly, I catch a glimpse through an open door. I can see Sleeping

Lady kneeling on the floor. Her bowed head is quivering as she sobs. After all these years, I can finally understand why the sad lady seems to cry at night—battling depression beneath the shadows of Denali has taking its toll on her.

Chapter 3

# *Andrea Alaskan Proprietress*

Andrea Altiery is in my dreams, and we are dangerously close to falling in love. In my dreams, as I look up into the night sky, I can see swirling, glittering ice dust that's falling all around me. There are hidden stars above these clouds that twinkle like silver. They smile down upon all that stand below this gathering dust, watching as it fluffs up around us. The more we all smile, the more it swirls downward, upon our lifted faces.

Soft bells ringing like a whistling wind cause me to look up to my right, where I can read Hilton in huge blue letters on the side of a tall building. This spot is strangely familiar to me. *Am I in Anchorage again? Is this Anchorage Alaska?* I turn slightly to my left, and immediately I am bathed in the glow of a reddish neon sign shaped like a big, old, antique box camera. Large, luminescent words above my upturned head, Stewart's Photo Shop, shine down upon me and illuminate the sidewalk all around.

I hear the soft, whistling bells again. Cautiously I turn; my eyes fall upon a spry elderly woman. She is elegant in appearance. The spry woman is walking a caribou on a long chain and leash. The caribou has long curled up hooves that clop at a steady pace as he walks. I can hear the woman yelling, "Star halt … Star halt." They both stop. Star the caribou turns his head to look at me. His eyes are bulging and droopy. Blinking at me, Star shakes his head, causing the Arctic bell string that is buckled around his girth to start ringing.

The fur on the elegant woman's hat begins to bristle in the breeze. Star the caribou stomps his right front foot, and he turns in my direction. Star is looking directly at me, snorting his caribou contempt in my face. The Arctic bell string the caribou is wearing starts ringing every time he stomps in my direction. He seems agitated; there is steam coming out of his nostrils. I start laughing as I walk around them. Suddenly I am overcome with a feeling of sadness for the caribou, because Star looks very lonely to me. The ringing thought that is bouncing through my mind is, *There will be no reindeer games for Star the caribou tonight.*

I continue on my quest. The sign on the next shop grabs my attention; my body stiffens. I stop and behold—a sign stenciled in bold gold letters. I read—"Andrea's Antique Jewelry." Suddenly I can feel a warm wave of familiar anxiety. Palpitations begin pulsing through my body. I know this place. It's been engraved in my heart for years. My head turns to my right, and in bold green letters on a sign for Stewart's Photo Shop, I can read, "Jade is the stone of heaven."

As I excitedly approach the door that goes into Andrea's Antique Jewelry shop, two shabby women, both dressed in black dresses, both with sad faces, try to stop me from entering the shop. They both reach out with decaying, bony fingers, trying to latch onto my clothes. I pull away and start jumping up and down to see over their heads into the store. I am standing on my tip toes but to no avail. I can't see past the two women with sad faces.

Suddenly the door to Andrea's Antique Jewelry shop opens. A strong wind exhales from inside the shop, and the two shabby women dressed in black step aside. They allow an exquisitely, vibrant woman to walk out onto the sidewalk. Without warning, the exquisite woman turns and glances my way. She smiles while nodding her head approvingly and seductively motions for me to follow her, her long red hair tempting and alluring.

I can hear a melodious series of chimes ringing in the background. They seem to be beckoning for the benevolent ones. The sound gently guides me back around toward the doorway again, like a subtle dance. The two women with sad faces are gone now, and I am looking at a beautifully stenciled fish image on the glass of the door. It could possibly be a Cook Inlet beluga whale—she is splashing in the chop, amid the pulse of her pod. Rushing, rippling tides pushing back against her tender flesh.

I catch a glimpse of the address above the door. It reads 533 W.4th Ave, Gallery Hours, Mon–Sat 11am–6pm. My eyes become moistened on the next words. I freeze as I behold the written name. A smile washes over me like the rising sun after a long, dark Arctic winter—the perceived warmth of those first rays as they creep above the far horizon. Written in an italicized, custom, freestyle font across the glass of the front door—Andrea Altiery—Proprietress. The letters are emboldened and made more prominent by turquoise glitter that is surrounded by a delicate white frost background.

As I eagerly push the front door open, I am immediately met by an elderly woman. She smiles and approaches me. She is explaining to me that the beautiful jewelry inside this shop is being made on location by the proprietress herself. I ask the woman her name, and she replies, "Hi, I'm Stacy." Stacy extends her delicate hand in my direction, "And your name is …?"

I gingerly take her hand. "Stacy, my name is Bob. Is Andrea in the shop today?" She coyly smiles at me over her right shoulder and nods her head for me to follow her down a long hallway. She has shaggy blonde hair with ginger highlights, and is wearing a pair of wolf eye earrings that are set in black onyx, dangling and delicious. Stacy leads me into a dark, intimate space, where I can see happy couples looking at sparkling diamonds and shiny pearls on glass shelves, dancing and delighted amid their heart's desires.

As we walk, Stacy explains to me that the proprietress is trying to evoke a feeling of past civilizations—she wants to remind us of the gems' natural origins, both ancient and humble. As we come into the next space, I am reading a sign that is painted on jade-tinted glass. Wedding Band Alcove is written in delicate pink-and-white lettering with a red rose backdrop. The Wedding Band Alcove has an abundance of cabinets that are covered with intricate canopies. They are all brimming and overflowing with sparkling diamonds and gems.

An overpowering aroma that is very familiar to me is being blown our way by a small fan that is sitting on a stool over in the corner. There's a humidifier that has essential oils added to it placed on the floor. As the vapors rise from the humidifier, the small fan sends the winds of passion our way. It's an encompassing aroma that encircles us—the smell of vanilla mixed with rose, infused with slight hints of lavender and lilac.

When I hear the sound of splashing water, I become caught in a whirlpool of emotions. Suddenly I find myself alone with a shimmering shadow. She grabs me by my hand and starts pulling me to follow her. The shadow leads me into a space where I can see a woman standing in the corner. She has her back turned to me. She has long, brown auburn hair that is flowing across her shoulders and back. The woman turns around and starts walking toward me. My whole body stiffens, and I freeze because it's Andrea Altiery—I have found her. I am overcome with elusive, evasive emotions as she moves toward me. Will she recognize me?

Today Andrea is wearing the pair of brown suede leather cowboy boots that are knee high; they have big laces that run the full length up the back of her calves. Her walk is graceful and smooth with a small bounce to it. Her head is slightly rocking back and forth with each step she takes as she approaches the counter area. Finally, after all these years, she approaches toward me.

I notice Andrea is holding a pencil in her left hand. She raises it to her lips as she looks down at the clipboard in her right hand. Frowning slightly, she looks up past me toward the front door of her shop. Following her gaze, I turn and look in the same direction when I hear the chimes on the front door start ringing. A group of enthusiastic young women come walking into the shop; all are giggling and pointing as they enter Andrea's shop.

With a thunderous shout, I call out to Andrea, hoping she hears the call of my lonely heart. One of the young women breaks off from the group and walks over toward me. The young woman stops and stands between Andrea and me. She is blocking my view of Andrea. I start waving both my hands above the young woman's head, indicating my desperate desire to get Andrea's attention. With fearful apprehension, I realize I have been waving in vain.

Today I find myself swimming through a crowd, pushing against the pulse of silt-laden tides. The proprietress herself didn't have time to see me today, yet I can still hear her soft voice, calling me, from another place, and another time. We will meet again on the waters someday, smiling and holding hands. Walking together through jade-laden gorges that reflect our radiant smiles, both bathed by prismatic sunsets, splashing across our eternal horizons ...

Chapter 4

# *Elusive Alaskan Proprietress*

Trembling in my sleep, I am dreaming. I find myself on a snow-covered street on a chilly, overcast morning, about to enter my hotel. As I walk in, there is a strange woman waiting in my hotel lobby, and she tries to convince me to leave the hotel with her. I have an overwhelming feeling that surges through me—if I decide to leave with her, the end results may become forbidding or even uninviting for me.

The telephone ringing loudly in my hotel room wakes me up to an uneasy feeling, which starts growing into worry as I reach out to answer the telephone. Jackie down at the front desk is calling me about a bicycle rental for today. She wants to know if I will be okay with an orange bicycle to ride, and I explain to her that she has called the wrong room. I am not looking to rent a bicycle today, I inform her. Jackie kindly laughs, apologizes, and wishes me happy thoughts throughout my day.

My shaving and showering completed, I stand in front of the window, ironing my clothes while watching the weather reports on the television. It looks like today is going to be great walking weather—fifty-five degrees and sunny in Anchorage, perfect weather for Alaska and to start my search for Andrea. I know it's all on a whim; all of it has been stimulated by some vivid dreams, this longing desire for Andrea that I have burning within me, lonely, wallowing in my desires, indulgent and unrestrained.

I begin searching the telephone book's white pages for her name, but I don't find an Andrea Altiery listed, so I check the yellow pages, looking for a business listing under Andrea's Antique Jewelry. Nothing is listed at all. An overwhelming feeling of emptiness washes over me. Suddenly I have a lack of meaning or purpose, a deep sense of nothingness.

I shake my foreboding feelings off and write down three potential jewelry stores that I can check into. I take my time looking at all the advertisements that have pictures or images in them. I am looking for a beluga whale mural stenciled on a door, but today it seems to be evading me. Elusive. Maybe tomorrow, in a different book or on another page.

The very first thing I'll do is walk the two blocks to 533 W.4th Ave. I saw this address in my dreams about Andrea's Antique Jewelry shop—that location is right here in the same neighborhood as my hotel. I step out into bright sunshine that's soothing on my face, but my body starts to tense while I am walking. *What do I say if Andrea is here? Will she remember me? Will she want to remember me? Will she want to see me again?* I have a lot of confused and conflicted thoughts wrestling for my mind's attention as I am walking.

When I get up on W.4th Avenue, I realize I need to eat. Luckily for me, the Downtown Cafe and Deli is right next door to Stewart's Photo Shop. It's busy in here this morning, but I luck out and get a small table right at the front window. A gorgeous waitress comes my way smiling.

"Hi, I'm Gail. Can I start you with coffee today?"

"Yes, and I am ready to order, Gail." As she is writing my order, I can't stop staring at her earrings. When Gail notices me staring at her earrings, I blush and quickly look back down at my menu.

Gail starts laughing while she is pushing her pencil behind her right ear. She starts explaining to me she is wearing a pair of handcrafted earrings and they are made out of woolly mammoth ivory. She shows me a beautifully scrimshawed scene of two beluga whales swimming under a full moon. Gail goes on to tell me the ivory is almost ten thousand years old and it was found right here in Alaska, up on the North Slope.

"Very nice. Where did you buy your earrings, Gail?" When Gail tells me she bought the earrings over at David's Jewelry store in the Northway Mall, my attention is piqued. She awakens something deep inside me that causes me to sit up sharply and stare at her. She seems startled by my quick movement and sudden glare. Taken aback, Gail quickly steps away from the table.

"I'm sorry, I didn't mean to scare you, Gail. I am looking for a lost friend, and I am going over to the Northway Mall later to browse in David's Jewelry store. The coincidence just caught me off guard for some reason." I tell her I need to step outside while my food is being prepared and excuse myself. "I've taken up to much of your time already, Gail."

Smiling, she responds to me, "No problem. Your food will be ready in ten minutes. Don't go far," while glancing curiously at me over her shoulder.

It's only a few steps over to 533 W.4th Ave. I walk past Stewart's Photo Shop while glancing up at the antique box camera neon sign. When I get to 533 W.4th Ave, nothing occupies the space. It's totally empty. A big red "Space for Rent" sign being held by twine is hanging crooked in the large window, a telephone number has been handwritten with red marker, and it's almost not legible now. The fading ink is bleeding, and trailing off into nothingness. I am suddenly overwhelmed with choking emotions. My mind becomes frozen in time. I am feeling queasy and faint. Suddenly my knees buckle beneath the weight of my emotional disintegration.

Embarrassment and humiliation. I lean against the window and start laughing hysterically. *What am I doing? What was I thinking? Andrea's long gone. Give it up. She's moved on.* Exhausted, I slowly trudge back into the Downtown Cafe and Deli to eat my food. Gail tells me they thought I wasn't coming back. "I couldn't forget about you, Gail. I couldn't abandon my only real friend in town now, could I?" Gail looks my way with a sad frown. I sit down to eat alone in my mental isolation. I have a crushed heart and a lonely mind, absorbed in my own shattered virtual reality.

As I am eating, I suddenly become flushed with anger at my situation. I try to convince myself that getting angry isn't bad. Anger is nothing more than a signal being sent to my brain that someone or something is doing something I don't like or agree with. Calm down, this desire I have to lash out right now is only my response to this anger. I dealt myself these cards. Now I need to play the hand. I must find a solution inside myself, look into my dreams and past my deceptions for the answers.

There's only one place in Anchorage where I can really gather my thoughts, and that's up on Arctic Valley Road, at the Arctic Valley overlook. I decide I am going to drive up there after I eat. I will suspend my search for Andrea for now. I need to rearticulate my thought process and give myself a much needed attitude adjustment while enjoying the views of Cook Inlet, Sleeping Lady, and distant mountain peaks that are snow covered and inviting to the weary eye.

As I drive through the Moose Run Golf course on Arctic Valley Road, I can see two bald eagles soaring together, high up in the sky, above me. You can't mistake a bald eagle's glide—the tips of their wings spreading into the wind as they turn, each individual feather grabbing and clinging to the currents as they hover. Eagle heads flinch, while piercing eyes gaze below, their cries echo as four wings fold in unison, and together they dive. With quivering bodies, unseen prey goes darting for the shadows, as fear begins pulsing through Arctic Valley.

Chapter 5

# *Precocious and Pregnant*

Tonight is for me. I am going out on the town, find some fun, and get out of my own head and into someone else's thoughts. Looking for something different, I find myself walking into the Gaslight Bar and Lounge at 721 W.4th Ave. They have a big mechanical riding bull in the middle of the floor. They also have pool tables and pinball machines. Tonight thick crowds are pushing through the doors searching for beer on tap.

Surprisingly I find a small round table in the middle of the crowd that is not taken. It has two empty chairs waiting to be occupied. A waiter immediately comes walking over to me and yells into my ear that his name is Kevin. "Are you waiting for anybody else?" he asks me. I shake my head no. Sadly he nods back as he takes my order. "Whiskey on the rocks. I need to hydrate. I had a tough day today," I explain to him. Kevin doesn't smile at me.

Appearing out of the crowd, two sexy women in tight jeans are walking toward me smiling, one of them pointing at the empty chair next to me, "Can we jump in here?" she asks me. "I'm Sharon, and this is my cousin Debbie."

"Hi, I'm Bob, and yes, please sit with me, ladies. Please sit yourselves down." I stand up so both women can sit. Nice that I am off to a fast start tonight, I'm thinking, as Sharon and Debbie get adjusted into their seats. I watch them as they arrange their accessories on the table top, both women getting comfortable while they are settling into their new space.

When I see the waiter Kevin, I motion him over to our table, emphatically and earnestly Sharon starts waving her hand back and forth for him to go away. She is laughing at me. "We always drink for free," she is yelling into my ear. Loud crowds are swarming all around us. "Huh, drink for free, what?" I yell back to her. Sharon, smiling, yells, "Watch this, Bob."

Both Sharon and her cousin Debbie get up; both women look back at me with sensual and alluring smiles as they start working the pulsing crowd. Both women start flipping their long black hair over their shoulders as they walk, gently placing hands on every guy they pass. Their tight jeans hugging at attractively curved hips, thin black belts neatly wrapping waists where jacket and jeans meet, my eyes hungrily watching them melt into the awaiting crowd.

Within twenty minutes, our table is full of cocktails and beers. I am on my third drink before Sharon and Debbie return to the table to sit back down with me. There is an amazing energy flowing out of these two women tonight, their long black hair with their dark charcoal eyes penetrating deep into my soul. The flow of their leisurely walk meandering through the thick crowd beckons to the wild within me becomes fiercely energizing and raw. I like these two women a lot.

Sharon leans into me and asks me if I want to leave with her, "Let's get out of here and enjoy the night," she shyly suggests.

I jump right in and respond, "Yes, let's go. Let's enjoy."

While Sharon is telling Debbie we are leaving together, an older lady emerges from the chaotic crowd and pulls me aside. She motions for me to lean down to listen to her. "Listen, my friend, these two are trouble," she explains while grinning at me, her missing front teeth giving her a cute, comical look. The older lady with missing teeth begins shaking her head back and forth saying, "No … no … no. Don't go," then she repeats it, "No … no … no. don't go."

Before I can respond, Sharon comes back over to me and starts feverishly pulling on me to follow her through the crowd. While I am looking back at the older lady, she gives me a sad grin. Her face is contorted and subdued. Seemingly dejected, she turns away from me and walks into the crowd as I get pulled into the night by a frenzied Arctic lynx.

When we finally step outside, there is a taxi parked right outside the Gaslight Lounge. Sharon walks over and starts tapping on the roof of the car. The driver leans down to look up at us through his windshield. As he rolls the window down, Sharon asks him, "Can you get us down to O'Malley Road and Lake Otis Parkway area?"

"Jump in and let's roll," he replies to us. We both hop into his car quickly. The driver reaches over and pushes something on the dashboard, causing a glowing, little blue light to come on. Our driver then quickly stomps on the gas pedal, his tires start spinning in the sand, and we get violently thrown back into our seats.

Sharon reaches over and grabs onto me. She pulls me into her and asks me if I like her smell as she lightly brushes her wrist across my nose. Sharon explains to me, "I go by a man's smell, his scent," while her eyes hungrily undress me, coaxing me, softly calling my name. I grab her head and pull it firmly into my nose while I deeply inhale her fragrance. She looks up at me and rubs her nose tip against my nose tip—we are smiling into each other's eyes. We both seem to understand without words what the essence of our love will become. It's in the aroma, the lingering scent that will remind us.

The taxi pulls us into a nice little place off Hane Street. As we pull in, there's a dirty dog chained to an old truck tire that's half buried in the ground. Sharon explains to me that she is dog sitting for her sister Sue. Sue is off to their village, visiting around with family and friends, up on the mighty Yukon River. "Have you ever been up on the Yukon?" Sharon asks me.

"No, I haven't," I reply, but I am thinking about the older woman's words of warning back at the Gaslight Lounge right now, not the Yukon river.

The dirty dog that's chained to the tire doesn't even glance our way. When we get out of the taxi, it's peering off into the distance, seemingly waiting for Sue's return. Sharon has chimes hanging all around her front porch area. A small breeze brings us a tinkling message of delight. The sound reaches out toward us as we approach the front door. One of the chimes in particular catches my attention—it's a bunch of sea shells, all of them shaped like killer whales. This particular chime is low frequency, melancholic, and deep toned, its robust bass sound echoing its boom of doom.

Sharon unlocks the front door, and I follow her in. We walk through a collection of sea glass and driftwood in her front alcove space, which is very curious and interesting. When we get to her living room area, Sharon wastes no time. She turns on me and pounces like a lynx. She jumps up onto me while ravenously kissing on my neck. We both fall back onto a red leather couch. We are both kissing furiously, while grabbing at each other's face and hair. We are clawing at each other, like frenzied wolverines in a lustful state; our continued existence seems to be at stake. Sharon starts moaning heavily into my ear, "Take me ... take me ... take me."

All of sudden Sharon punches me in my face very hard with intent to hurt. Stunned from the punch, I rock back away from her. She starts screaming, "Rape ... Rape ... Rape," while furiously kicking at me with her painted toe nails. Not really being sure what I should do, I jump off the couch and start frantically looking around the room. The feeling of intense fear that is welling up inside me explodes into complete and utter terror, when I hear Sharon screaming over and over again, "Rape … Rape … Rape."

I have an immediate need to get out of this house, when suddenly and explosively a person comes out of nowhere, running full speed across the room at me like a football linebacker. Their head ducked down, they are coming in for the kill on me. The running body smashes into me, slamming us both against a wall near the front door. My head is jolted by the collision. I am now almost out the door. I have just one more assailant to get through when I turn to face my attacker.

I find myself looking into the eyes of a mad woman. Her face is flushed with anger. She has an evil grimace—lips curled, teeth clenched, braids of her hair bouncing into my face and blinding me as she swings hammer fists down on me. Wow, this lady is strong, and she is punching me with some fury. I need to break contact quickly and flee, run out the door and not look back.

I didn't come here looking for any trouble tonight, but trouble has found me. I am screaming, "Ma'am calm down … ma'am calm down," directly into the mad woman's face. As I push her off and away from me, I notice Sharon is watching us from the shadows, and she is screeching, "Get him … get that sucker good."

As I burst through the front door, the dog that's chained to the half-buried truck tire starts howling at me as I run by him. He seems to be howling in agony; he knows my pain. I can hear Sharon and the mad woman both yelling out the door behind me, "You ain't got no speed, sucker." As I continue to run through a neighbor's yard, a heavy tree branch slams into my teeth. My hand instinctively goes up to the searing pain, and I find myself looking down at a bloody hand.

It wasn't a long run, but I must be getting older, because I find myself leaning against the light pole at the corner of O'Malley Road and Lake Otis Parkway, trying to catch my breath. Maybe it was the momentary terror rushing through my mind and body and clenching at my gut that's causing me to gasp for air. Or maybe, it was my serendipitous encounter with the wayward tree branch slamming into my teeth. A deep, hysterical laughter keeps me leaning against the light pole for a while. I am just glad to be alive.

I gather myself up and run across O'Malley Road to start hitchhiking. I am hoping to get a ride up along Lake Otis Parkway so I can get back into downtown Anchorage. The third car that comes along pulls over about fifty feet up the road past me. I can see two people are sitting up front, and the back seat is full of household items. They have a California license plate on their car, and as I quickly run up to the car, the driver motions for me to climb into the back seat. He yells back to me that the door is unlocked, to please jump in.

Jumping into a back seat with three laundry baskets full of laundry and a bunch of kids' toys cluttering the floor really doesn't bother me. I am just glad to be getting out of this area. The guy driving asks me where I am going and replies, "Cool. We are heading over toward Government Hill. We can drop you off as we pass through the downtown area, man." The lady with him is smiling over her left shoulder at me.

She reaches back to shake my hand. "Hi, I'm Charlene. This is Bruce. We just got into town from California."

"Hi, I'm Bob. I'm trying to escape back into downtown."

Charlene and Bruce curiously glance at each other. Bruce yells back, "Hey, Bob, need a beer?" while he is looking back at me in his rearview mirror.

"Absolutely," I respond quickly. Bruce puts his right directional on and immediately pulls the car over.

He yells back to me, "Jump out, bro." I unbuckle my seatbelt and follow him to the back of their car.

Bruce is smiling, "You're going to love this, man." He pops the trunk open, and inside there is a cooler. Inside the cooler, we have beer and various small bottles of hard liquor on ice. Let the fun begin, I am thinking. Yes, let's drink. I grab a cold beer to go. I ask him if Charlene needs anything, but he explains to me she is pregnant, and she can't drink and won't drink. Bruce opens a larger bottle and takes a vigorous swig. He shakes his head and hands me the bottle. I grab the bottle and tilt it back. Liquid fire is flowing down my throat.

When I get back into the car, I congratulate Charlene on her upcoming baby, and she seems appreciative for my thoughts. She smiles. Bruce starts driving a little wildly. Regardless, we make it to the intersection of Lake Otis Parkway and E.15th Avenue at Merrill Field. As we turn left onto E.15th Avenue, I look up to my right, and I can see a large sign that reads Merrill Field Airport. Up on the small hill, over to the right, I can see some small planes sitting along an empty fence line. Two of the planes are blue, one is red, one is yellow, and I can't make out that last one.

Bruce probes me a little bit, then inquires if I am into smoking bud, and if so, would I like to take the ride with him and Charlene over to Government Hill while he meets up with someone. "We can smoke after I meet up with these people," Bruce explains to me.

"Sure I'm in. Let's do it, but can we stop and grab another beer first?"

Bruce puts on his directional again, but this time we pull into a parking lot—it's safer in here, he explains. Before we start getting back into the car, Bruce asks me if I want to sit up front with him and Charlene and hang out with the grown-ups.

I tap his roof and reply, "Sure thing. Thanks, Bruce."

Once we start driving again, it doesn't take us long to get into downtown Anchorage. We drive 15th Avenue, all the way to A Street. A Street is a straight shot through downtown, up into the Government Hill area. I know this road well—I have been on it many times in the past. When we get to the intersection of A Street and 5th Avenue, the traffic light is red, and we need to stop the car. This seems to irritate Bruce. Frenzied, he starts pounding his steering wheel with a clenched fist. This causes Charlene to push snugly, up against my left shoulder.

His irritation turns into annoyance because of the long wait, so when the light turns green, he pounds down hard on the gas pedal. We are driving very fast on A St as we approach the upcoming intersection with 4th Avenue. Suddenly, the upcoming traffic light turns red. Instead of stopping, Bruce decides to hammer the gas pedal and drive right through the red light. Charlene and I both brace for the impending doom.

The car does a little bounce off the ground as we fly across 4th Avenue, both airborne and crazy eyed. Fortunately for everyone involved, we do not collide with any people, cars, or objects. As we land, the car madly and repeatedly bounces up and down along A St. Charlene is frantically screaming. She is shrieking in Bruce's face to pull over and stop the car. Her bony elbows are digging deeply into my ribs as she frantically pulls on him.

Bruce has no choice; he has to stop the car. An Anchorage police cruiser had been parked on E.4th Avenue, facing west, toward the A Street intersection. They saw us airborne, flying through the intersection, and now they are in hot pursuit of us. They have lights flashing, sirens blazing. Look out, here they come in full force.

The police chase us across 3rd Avenue. Bruce violently jerks on the steering wheel as he pulls the car over into a gravel bus stop area just before the overpass. Bruce starts swearing. He is telling both Charlene and me that he can't get arrested for drunk driving again and he has two prior driving while intoxicated charges on his record. He starts pounding on the dashboard with hammer fists of fury again.

Honestly, I'm in shock as the Anchorage police surround our car. Three police cruisers are on the scene. I am being regaled with a colorful account of flashing lights.

Passersby are glaring at us as they slowly drive by. A tall police officer gets out of his police cruiser with a piercing flashlight. He starts to direct the traffic around the sudden obstruction. A second police officer walks up to the car and taps on the driver's side window. He loudly yells for Bruce to step out of the vehicle. "Sir, we need you to step out of the vehicle as safely as possible."

Bruce obeys and exits the car, with his hands up. I can hear him telling the second police officer he doesn't want any trouble today. A third police officer jumps on Bruce's wrist and twists him around, while the second police officer gets his handcuffs on him. They are both yelling at him, "Don't resist us ... don't resist us. You found trouble today ... don't resist us," while they roughly push him down onto the hood of the car.

When Bruce looks in through the windshield at Charlene and me, my heart sinks, as I am overwhelmed by a feeling of impending doom. Feeling like I am stranded on a skiff, I turn to look out my passenger side window. I can see a familiar tree line below me in a park—it's Barrow Park. I used to sit down there alone at night and ponder my life's insanities. *I remember a time sitting there with a friend. Both our hearts were bonding as we laughed. Andrea's heart pulse was a staccato rhythm that day, heavily vibrating through my trembling finger tips. As I gently clasped the soft skin on her muscular neck, we were looking deeply and longingly into each other's eyes. We slowly kissed ...*

There's an Anchorage police officer knocking on my window, and he is asking me to step out of the vehicle.

"Sir, please step out of the vehicle. He wants you to drive his car." The police officer is waving the ignition keys in the air—huh, what? My heart stops. My first problem, I have been drinking, and it's a high probability I am beyond the legal limit and would fail a sobriety test. My second problem, this police officer is going to hand me the keys to someone else's car. No way, no way, I can't let this happen to me today.

To avoid arrest, I indulge Mr. Police Officer, and I slowly step out of the car with my hands raised in the air. A playful thought comes to me, and I start acting like nature is screaming. I start hopping up and down, telling the police I really need to go to the bathroom, it's an emergency. Every police officer starts laughing, and they have me run down the embankment next to a concrete wall to take care of the business.

I am shaking my head in total disbelief at my sudden circumstances. I didn't have to go to the bathroom. I just needed time to think. *Should I try to run? Should I walk back up and tell the police I was just hitchhiking and want no part of this*, be honest with them?

Slipping on the wet grass, I make my way back up to the car that's surrounded by police cruisers. Bruce is handcuffed and sitting in the backseat of one cruiser. I can see Charlene sitting like a statue in the car that picked me up hitchhiking. I don't think the poor girl has moved since the car has been stopped. Good for her. Protect your baby, Charlene, like a mother grizzly bear would.

When I get back to the car, the Anchorage police don't ask me to show them my license; they don't ask me if I've been drinking. As one of the officers tries to hand me the car keys, I put my hands up while I'm explaining, "Officers, I can't drive this car. I've been drinking. I really shouldn't take the keys.

Can his girlfriend drive?"

"No, he wants you to drive the car," an officer responds matter of factly. "Please take the keys and move the car off the shoulder for us. And have a good night, sir."

As soon as I get into the car, Charlene slides over and grabs my right arm, "I am so embarrassed, Bob. I am so sorry for all of this. Please forgive me."

I respond, "Charlene, calm down. Please relax. Breathe. We are all right. We are good kid." I figure the best plan is to take A Street and get off at the next exit. Then we can drive down into the Ocean Dock Road area. This will allow me to circle us back around into the downtown area and get us into my hotel, hopefully get us to safety. Historic Anchorage Hotel, here we come, and we're coming in, shaken to the bone.

Charlene and I have our feet up on the ottoman in my room. We are both in total disbelief but glad to be safe for the night. Charlene uses the phone and calls the Anchorage police. They inform her they will release Bruce in the morning, but not before 9:15 a.m., she gets told. Charlene is very appreciative of me having her stay with me. She explains to me that she can't afford a room on her own. I explain to her that I couldn't let a pregnant woman sleep in her car, parked in the back of a windy, dusty parking lot somewhere, afraid and all alone.

I tell Charlene she can sleep on the only bed, so I grab the extra blanket and pillows from the closet to make a nest for myself on the floor. She begins to beg me to sleep in the bed with her. "I need to cuddle with you tonight … I need you to hold me, Bob." I give her a small laugh, then politely decline her invitation to get up into the bed with her. Charlene's blonde hair is in two big braids with red ribbons, her face is strongly freckled, her pink lips are pouting. Suddenly, she sits up to glare down at me.

"You're really going to sleep on the floor? You're really going to leave me up here all alone?" Charlene grabs a pillow and throws it at me, yelling, "Get lost, dude … get lost tonight" She abruptly slams herself back down into the mattress, then pulls the blanket over her entire body. She is yelling, "You're so unreal … unreal, dude. Go back to the East Coast where you belong … out here it's free love."

As I lie back into my blanket, and pillow nest, on the cold, hard wood floor of my hotel room, I can feel the hard wood floors, creaking and groaning from the gusting winds outside. I am slightly puzzled, maybe even a little perplexed, as I ponder how I have allowed a feisty pregnant woman to steal my hotel room from me this evening, leaving me lying on the floor. It leaves me feeling like a savage beast, whose destiny is to crawl among the crumbs, always grasping with raw, bloody fingers for my heart's longing desires.

# Chapter 6

# *Andrea's Daughter Andromeda*

Wake-up couldn't have come soon enough for me this morning. I am eagerly anticipating the exit of Charlene from my bathroom. Right now she is in there, dry heaving through a severe episode of morning sickness. I had to help her out of bed and into the bathroom, she was so unsteady on her feet, her face was white, she was sweating profusely, and her body was trembling. *I really hope I will not be delivering a baby this morning in my hotel room. I am not prepared for that at all, and it wouldn't be fair to the baby.*

Charlene, still unsteady on her feet, stumbles out of the bathroom and splashes herself back into the bed. She asks me if I can let her sleep longer, "Give me like three hours if possible, OK. Can you, please?"

I respond, "Listen, you look like you need to eat, orange juice for sugar ..." my voice trails off.

Charlene puts her hands up while shaking her head no, "Just the thought of food is gagging me, just leave me alone, before I puke."

I reply, "Ok listen, here's the deal, Charlene. I am leaving for three hours exactly. When I come back to the hotel, please be gone from my room. If you need to order anything, you can charge it to my room's account." Charlene's arms are folded tightly across her chest, and her lips are curled into a snarling glare, as I speak with her. "Listen, Charlene, I need you to be gone when I get back here, and good luck rounding up your buddy Bruce from the local police corral. Please be gone for me, ok?"

I abruptly exit my hotel room. I am snarling loudly to no one in particular. "Wow, I can't believe this situation. Unreal."

Out in the hallway, I bump into an older couple waiting at the elevator doors. They are loudly arguing over a piece of paper that the woman is holding. The older man is trying to pull the paper out of her hand. They both wrestle back and forth with it. "Give me this."

"No, keep your hands off it."

"I'm asking you to give me the tickets."

"No, you never trust me to do anything," the woman resentfully snorts toward the man. My head hanging low, I sullenly walk by them.

I am eager to take the quick walk back over to 533 W.4th Ave first thing this morning, take a look around, and slow it down so I can process all my thoughts. My dream about Andrea's Antique Jewelry shop was vivid enough for me to fly five thousand miles on a whim, looking for a girl with a smile and a plan. I feel it would behoove me to analyze and dissect that dream. The walk from my hotel takes me about three minutes, and before I know it, I am standing in front of 533 W.4th Avenue, downtown Anchorage Alaska for the second time on this trip.

Again, today it's an empty store front, with dingy glass that's cracked, gloomy, and drab. The big, red, "Space for Rent" sign, held by twine, is still hanging crooked in the large window. I look a little closer this time. I push my face against the glass to look inside the window, and down on the floor of the empty store, I can see a pile of old newspapers that are starting to turn yellow. Inside the window I am watching a fly caught in a spider web struggling for its survival. Behind me, car tires squeal. The screech causes me to jump.

Looking across the street, my eyes fall on flower pots that are hanging on light poles, I look down to park benches and green lawns offering public serenity. There's a log cabin visitors center across the street, which is covered with a sod roof. My eyes freeze on the log cabin with the sod roof. An overwhelming feeling of familiarity has me recalling my dream about Andrea's Antique Jewelry shop. In that dream, Andrea's shop attendant, Stacy, had spoken with me about the gems in the proprietress's shop being of *natural origins, both ancient and humble.*

With sudden clarity, I realize a sod roof is of natural origins, both ancient and humble. Is this why I was brought here, to behold the sod roof? Now my memories become more focused and clear. I remember a warm, sunny day, back in the spring of 1981. I had been walking through this exact spot, but I was on the other side of the street. A beautiful girl had called to me from the lawn as I was walking by. She was sitting over near some birch trees that are behind the log cabin.

She waves me over with a friendly smile. She is wearing a brown cowboy hat with a curled up brim, faded denim jacket, and blue jeans to match. She has two small bags lying next to her feet, and her two shoes are lying partially over her two bags.

We shake hands but never exchange our names, just smiles and words. She is reading a book about parenting. I ask her if she is pregnant, and she replies, "No," with a shy laugh. I ask her if she wants me to sit down and talk. She replies, "Yes, please sit down with me." We have a nice visual vantage point from here looking back toward 4th Ave. Stewart's Photo Shop is in the background, offering us the ability to stop time. We can archive small glimpses of our dreams if we choose to, sharing intimate moments that are forever frozen in time with our future.

As I am taking my seat, the friendly lady wearing the cowboy hat asks me if I like the rock band Aerosmith. I respond yes.

She smiles and slaps me on my left shoulder, telling me, "Dream on, my friend." The smiling lady then asks me if I want to have children someday.

I respond, "Yes, I do, and hopefully a daughter."

She responds to me, "No way … I want to have a daughter also." Realizing we both share the dream of having a daughter, we smile and slap hands.

I can hear the smiling lady explaining to me that she has always wanted to name her daughter Andromeda. Violently, my head snaps up. I look her directly into her face. She pulls back, startled, but still smiling at me. I begin to explain, "No way, I have been telling people for years that I want to name my daughter Andromeda. No way, really, are you for real right now?" Both of us are amazed. Our faces mirror bonding smiles, reflecting.

She asks me if I have time to hear about her visions and her dreams, for her daughter Andromeda's future.

I reply "Yes, of course I'll listen … it's almost like I have to now. I feel compelled." We continue to converse, while she conveys upon me her dream.

"I want to give birth to a daughter. Her name is going to be Andromeda. Andromeda will have auburn hair and sparkling green eyes. I want both of her eyes to be the same intense color. She's going to love mystical, silver beluga whales, and purple sea nymphs. Her favorite colors being both purple and silver."

I encourage her to continue, "That's a beautiful daughter you'll have … I'm sure her father is going to be proud of her."

"On Andromeda's bedroom door, a large purple heart will be hanging. It will have silver letters that spell out 'Enchanted Land of Dreams,' and the edges of the letters will be enhanced with turquoise glitter," she explains to me. I nod approvingly as she continues to speak. "Our house is going to be over on W.10th Avenue next to the Delaney Park Strip. We will be able to walk along Beech Lane, over to W.11th Ave. That will be our short cut over to the Westchester Lagoon area, and the railroad tracks."

"I am going to be painting the house pearl white, with jade green trim. I am having a black metal roof put on it for these Alaskan winters. I want to protect my assets and my family."

I reply to her, "I can understand what you're telling me. I like your vision. Please continue for me," as I smile at her.

She soothingly looks into my eyes, coaxing and tugging on my heart strings. She takes her cowboy hat off, and casually tosses it onto her bags, while she continues to stare at me.

"Andromeda has an exotic fish tank that rests on a black marble table. She has schools of jewel cichlid and neon tetra dancing in the swirl, "vibracious" plants twisting in the current, and glass whales covering the bottom. She has a blue light that glows from above. It's embracing and serene." *I notice the smiling lady is wearing a petite, fish-shaped gold necklace. It's lying across lightly tanned skin. The necklace is exquisite.*

"We drive in a white pickup truck that has a winch on the front bumper. In the bed of the pickup truck I have a tool box that also acts as a bench to sit on when we take scenery breaks. Andromeda loves to take her scenery breaks. Besides, we have to take scenery breaks, it's going to be a family rule." She continues talking, "One of Andromeda's favorite rides is driving up onto Arctic Valley Road, as we slowly drive back down the mountain side. She loves to have me stop at the overview pullout."

This grabs my attention. I excitedly explain to the smiling lady in the cowboy hat that I am stationed over at Fort Richardson, we are on Arctic Valley Road all the time. "I love it also. It's an amazing area up there. You're a soldier?" she asks me with surprise. "Yes, ma'am," I drawl. She laughs and reaches out to slap me on my left shoulder. In unison we both start saying, "I love the view of Sleeping Lady, no way." We slap hands smiling.

She continues, "Andromeda also loves looking across to Sleeping Lady. She likes to snuggle with me as we whisper our thoughts of love, both our love for each other, and her future loves yet to come." I nervously and gently put my hand on her foot as she speaks. She doesn't pull her foot away; instead she pushes it firmly against my hand. She wiggles her toes against my fingers. Her wool sock is soft and warm against my hand.

"Andromeda and myself like to hold hands while watching the purple sunsets that ripple across the waters of Cook Inlet, distant mountain peaks beckoning to the wild within our spirits. We watch airplanes that land from faraway places, carrying their precious loads of dreams, hopes for the future, I always tell Andromeda." My emotions are choking me now as she speaks. We longingly look into each other's eyes, while staring blindly into each other's souls.

"That's an amazing dream you have, young lady … I am moved by your words." I start to stand up, getting ready to leave, but find myself not really wanting to leave this place. I look around at the log cabin with the sod roof, the green lawn with the inviting benches, Stewart's Photo Shop off in the distance watching us, stalking us, waiting to capture us unexpectedly, and freeze us together forever in time.

My gaze comes back to the smiling woman in the cowboy hat. I reach out to shake her delicate but strong hand. She reaches up, and we slap hands instead. "I hope to run into you again someday, maybe we can get to know each other a little better," she responds with a gracious grin.

"Sounds great, I can't wait," I reply. As I am walking backward away from the smiling lady in the cowboy hat, my overimaginative waves flutter back toward her, when suddenly my mind begins to indulge in a daydream.

In this daydream this happens: *I am seeing a young girl sitting on the lap of her mother. The young girl has auburn hair and sparkling green eyes, her mother has long-flowing, brown auburn hair, and she is wearing a brown cowboy hat with a curled brim. They both turn to face me as I enter the sunroom. Together, they both smile at me. My wife reaches up for my hand, and my daughter loudly calls my name.*

# Chapter 7

# Tough Alaskan Love

I love being out here at Point Woronzof during the early mornings. It's truly a magical spot. This morning as I pull into the parking lot, a young bull moose is grazing the tree line along a walking trail. We have clear skies looking out across Cook Inlet. The sky is glowing purplish pink as the morning grows. In the distance, two fishing trawlers are pushing up Knik Arm toward the Port of Anchorage. There's a large flock of sea gulls trailing above each boat. I can hear their cries in the distance as they swarm.

I try to keep my distance from a beat-up, dented van that's parked in the corner of the parking lot. It's a yellow Dodge van with hints of rust around every edge. It has an Oregon license plate attached to it, and the back bumper is made of wood planks tied onto the van with ropes. They have reflectors duct taped onto the bumper for utility purposes. The windows on the side are covered by a sheet hanging over them. It's rolled up in the windows to hold it in place. It looks like Scoobie-Doo cartoon sheets, and Scoobie-Doo doesn't seem to be smiling at anyone today.

Back in 1982 during the week of the Fourth of July, a group of guys and myself were on the beach below. We had spent several days gathering driftwood to use as fuel for our beach fire, and had hidden the wood among the boulders at the base of the water tank down on the beach, our hope being that the tides wouldn't grab it away from us before we could burn it during our upcoming midnight beach party. We needed to keep the sea from reclaiming our caches of wooden treasure.

We got down onto the beach about 9:30 p.m. that night. The sun was still pretty high in the sky. We carried two coolers full of beer, water, and juices. One of the guys had brought several lawn chairs with him, and a very large radio for our audio entertainment. Surprisingly our wood was all still there, and more had drifted in for us to gather and burn, blessings from the wood gods.

The tide was still low, and the water line was a long way down the rocky shore. Everyone agreed it was best to build our fire up high near the rocks along the banking. We would let the rising tides come back up to us, calling at our feet, carrying their messages with them from far away shores. We start making a batch of jungle juice, it's made with Everclear, 190 proof, 95 percent alcohol by volume, mixed with grape juice—pretty nasty stuff.

I spit my first sip of jungle juice out onto the fire, causing the flames to flash up high. Everybody in the group starts laughing at me and pounding on my back.

The music gets turned up to The Doors singing "Come on baby, light my fire / Let's try to set the night on fire." I join in with the laughing and jumping around, my ankle suddenly rolls, and I collapse down onto the rocks, falling very hard. The whole group begins to laugh harder. They all start screaming "Come on baby, light my fire," while pointing accusing, unwashed fingers down into my contorted, upturned face.

Hours later as the skies darken and the moon starts to rise above the inlet, high tide has pushed the rolling waves right up into our camp, and we have to move all our gear back along the banking behind us. As I listen, I can hear stones tumbling as the waves wash them back down into the sea. It's a musical thumping that reaches into a crescendo, calling out for me to follow its echo down into the shadows beneath the surface of the water.

Seven people including myself are sitting in a single file line along the water's edge, our knees are pulled up to our chins and we are all staring silently out toward the water. We seem to be waiting in suspense for some unseen presence. Our driftwood fire is reflecting warmth across our backs, there's just a hint of our fire's light splashing across the edge of the water's surface, it dances back and forth over shiny rocks along the shore.

*We all hear the splashing at the same time. In unison we all look to our left when we realize the splashing is a pod of Cook Inlet beluga whales slowly swimming by us. The whales are very close to us, they are hugging tight into the shore. We can see their long backs, no dorsal fins, as they glide by us. We can hear their blowholes opening so they can take in big gulps of air as they slide back beneath the surface of the water. As they come back up, they turn their heads and look at the shore. Their used up air is being spouted back into the atmosphere. Salty, searing tears suddenly well up in my eyes.*

Harsh, loud voices, arguing, bring me back into the moment. Five people are walking up toward the parking lot from the beach below. I can see them coming up the trail that leads down to the beach. None of them look happy at all. There's two ladies who are pushing on each other and swearing. Both of them are wearing orange bandanas. One of the guys is swigging from a huge bottle. His pants are falling down below his waist. The two ladies in orange bandanas turn on him, yelling, "Share the booze."

"We wanna get plastered," they say.

They walk over to the yellow Dodge van, which has hints of rust around every edge, the van with the Oregon license plate. All of a sudden, one of the three guys grabs the taller women by the back of her collar, he pushes her head forcibly against the van face first. I hear the thud of her head banging against metal. He starts yelling with some venom, snarling at her, "Take that, big mouth. Take that." The shorter lady starts viciously kicking him in his shins, screaming, "Let her go … let her go, you bully."

Without warning, I have become a witness to a vicious assault in the shadows of the Sleeping Lady. I can see Sleeping Lady's longing glance come my way—she is searching for a solution. I decide to exit my vehicle, move in their direction, and get involved, I yell out to the assailant while I am walking toward him. "Hey, you, let her go … get your hands off her, now." He lets her go, and all five people turn to face me, all three guys glaring with evil grimaces. The women seem to have a glimmer of hope as they watch me approach the group.

The big angry guy who was assaulting the lady storms toward me like a charging grizzly bear, up on the Big Susitna River during king salmon season, nostrils flaring, his big booze nose shiny red. I segregate him away from his group of friends, and possibly any caches of weapons that may be stored in the van, by walking to the right side of the parking lot. Waving for him to follow me, I loudly taunt, "It gets real over here … get real on me, buddy. Come on."

As the angry man rushes in on me, he snarls, "You got something to say to me? Don't even think about it."

I turn in a semicircle so he has his back to the water. I can see a flock of geese flying by out over Cook Inlet behind him, their calls drifting up to us on the winds.

I focus on the angry man and reply, "Listen, man, if you touch her one more time while I'm here, there's going to be a price to pay. You got it?"

He gets in close and towers over me, while glaring down with a menacing look, "Who's writing that check, wise guy?" he growls, down into my face. I can smell the stale alcohol saturating his breath.

I forcibly step into his personal space. He pulls back startled, but he firmly holds his ground. I look up at him, "Listen, big boy, you can make your move on me, you can make your move on one of your buddies, but if you touch any of the women again while I am here, there's going to be a price to pay!"

To make sure he understands my message, I scream a deep, guttural, throaty, scream. It wells up from the pit of my stomach, my diaphragm expands, "NOW STAND DOWN. STAND DOWN." He quickly throws his hands up, begins to furiously nod his head up and down like he completely understands my message, then slowly backs away from me, with his weary eyes leering.

I need to escape this emotional chaos that I have un-expectedly been thrust into this morning, so as I am walking toward my car, I indulge myself into a daydream. *I find myself out on a busy, crowded street. It's a hot summer night in downtown Anchorage. I am standing alone in front of a jewelry shop door, staring at a beluga whale mural on the door.*

# Chapter 8

# *Fluttering Arctic Tern*

My foot is heavy on the gas pedal of my red Pontiac Grand Am as I pass the yellow van on my way out of Point Woronzof's parking lot. All five people are looking at me as I wildly beep my horn, while pointing at the big angry guy. Fire is steaming out of my eyes. They shattered my tranquility, and now I am angry. I drive the three miles on Northern Lights Blvd to Wisconsin Street in a blind rage, white stars are clouding my peripheral vision like fireworks exploding, an ACDC song is blaring out of the car stereo speakers, "No stop signs, no speed limit, nobody's gonna slow me down."

Continuing my erratic drive on West Northern Lights Blvd, I pass through Benson Blvd onto East Northern Lights Blvd, until I reach Bragaw Street. The left flowing traffic is built up at the lights. It looks like there is a large scale event happening at East Anchorage High School this morning—time for me to relax, be very cautious. There are young people swarming everywhere as I turn left, and pass up through the school's campus area. The little balls of hazard are running around clamoring for attention, distraught parents looking frazzled.

I have severe hunger pangs that have been tearing across my midsection. Grimacing, I see a Denny's up ahead on my right—*nice, let me pull in here*—just in time, I need a break. As I pull into an empty parking lot, there's a newspaper box that's hanging open, and its contents are being pulled out onto the ground by swirling breezes. There's a lone raven sitting on top of a light pole looking down at me as I park my car, his feathers are fluttering in the wind.

As I enter the restaurant, a couple of women with tired faces are seated at the breakfast bar. It's cluttered with baskets of single serve jellies, sugar packets, and bottles of condiments. There's a server seated in the front area who ignores me as I walk past her. I need to use the restroom and then find a table in a corner. I want to isolate myself from as many staring eyes as possible this morning, so I can drown my sorrows in hot, black, bitter coffee.

After I get seated, the server whom had ignored me comes over with water, a menu, and she introduces herself, "Hi, I'm Rhonda. I'll try my best to take care of you," she smiles.

I like her nose ring. It's a dark emerald green. Rhonda sees me staring at it and blushes. Feeling awkward and embarrassed, I quickly drop my eyes down to my menu. Rhonda asks me for my drink order. "Coffee, hot and black with a glass of grape juice if you have any, please."

"We can do that, sugar." I get a big smile from Rhonda as she walks away.

A loud banging sound, followed by a crash, coming from the front entrance area causes me to spin around in my seat. An older man has just fallen down as he was walking in. It looks like he tripped over his own untied shoe laces. I start to stand up, maybe he needs help. Suddenly, one of the women with a tired face runs over to help him—she steadies him, helps him grab the door handle.

Rhonda is making her way back with my food, so I take my seat again. She is looking back over her left shoulder, while shaking her head in the direction of the doorway drama that is still being played out in the background. "Wow, I am very sorry for that sir, please don't be mad at me," Rhonda teasingly comments. She places my plate onto the cluttered table, and I can see a generous amount of unevenly distributed food looking sullenly back at me.

"Rhonda, it's not your fault, you did your job—my food is here." I smile up at her and notice she is wearing a pair of very dainty feather earrings. "Rhonda, would you mind telling me where you got your earrings? They are beautiful."

"Glad you like them. I bought them right around the corner from here at the Northway Mall. Probably like eight months ago now. They are Arctic tern tail feathers. Kinda spendy, but unique to Alaska."

Rhonda's smile is bedazzling, her bright blue eyes are shadowed by long, luscious eye lashes, and house an eternal twinkle.

"Wow, did you say Northway Mall? Did you get them at David's Jewelers?" I ask her.

Rhonda, with a beaming smile, replies, "Yes, David's Jewelers. How did you know that?"

"I'm going over there when I leave here, I am looking for a long lost friend, her name is Andrea Altiery. Andrea is skilled at making custom jewelry, so I am just checking around, going into different jewelry shops around Anchorage."

"I'm sorry, I don't know any Andrea. My friend Jessica works part time over there, though. Maybe she could help you." I sit up. I am very interested in having someone to possibly speak with who is in the jewelry business, maybe get into a casual conversation about Andrea. I need someone whom I can use as a sounding board about my thoughts, and my dreams—am I insane for allowing myself to be driven by my emotions? My thought process is choked with torrential waves of fear, the fear of never being able to find that treasure of my burning heart's desire.

I bring myself back into the moment. I respond to Rhonda, "Sweet I have an Anchorage connect. Do you think Jessica is working today?" I think, *would I freak her out if I walk in asking for her? She's going to call the police on me, isn't she? Why would anyone want to speak with me? I'm crazy, it feels like my mind is going to explode.*

Rhonda responds, "Yes, she is, tell her I sent you, and tell her she better take care of you."

I reply, "Ok Miss Rhonda, will do."

As I leave the restaurant, the lone raven that was sitting on top of the light pole is hopping on the ground, along the driver's side of my car. With a lone squawk, the raven croaks, "Kraa" into my face. His head is tilted, with one eye peering up at me. Shooing him back with both hands, I quickly jump into my car and lock the door. My fear is starting to turn into panic as I struggle to get the ignition key inserted. I've been accosted by a relentless raven strutting at my car door.

It's a short drive over to David's Jewelers, but I keep ducking down and looking out my windshield, my eyes scanning the top of every light pole for a lone raven. I keep looking into my rearview mirror to see if the raging raven is chasing me. His spreading wings will cast long shadows beneath him, blocking the sun as he swoops down across my windshield. Dark shadows engulf me, causing me to pound my brake pedal down, pumping on the brake, pumping my car to a stop.

By the time I pull into the Northway Mall parking lot, I am a raving lunatic, my life is in a spiral, black feathers are clouding my vision. The parking lot is extremely busy, but a kind, older woman, in a black, Ford Ranger pickup truck allows me to pull into her parking space. Waving, she smiles through her dark sunglasses toward me. I acknowledge her courtesy, my own smile, with an enthusiastic wave, back in her direction.

David's Jewelers is an amazingly inviting space. As I enter, an older gentleman is busy helping a young, happy couple look at a variety of jewelry. I can see into a glass room that is secured from the outside. Inside there are multiple jewelers engaged in different stages of fine jewelry production. One of the jewelers is looking closely at a gem through an eye glass, she is wearing gloves, she has a mask over her mouth and nose. I am spellbound as I watch her. She is meticulous in her movements, graceful in her disposition.

She has auburn hair that hangs gently over her white smock. I can see an identification card hanging on a green lanyard from her muscular neck. An older woman approaches me. "Hello, can I be of assistance this morning? My name is Ruth." Her delicate hand is extended, so I gently take it into mine. "Hi, I'm Bob. Thank you, Ruth. Yes, you can be of help. I am looking for an employee named Jessica. Would she happen to be working today, Ruth?"

Ruth turns and points toward the meticulous woman with auburn hair working in the glass room. "That would be Jessica right there, Bob," Ruth replies. My heart begins to melt within me, burning memories of Andrea come flooding back to me. I have strong hopes Jessica can help me in my search for Andrea. Please let her have some answers for me, maybe I'll finally find a solution to this agonizing emotion filled puzzle. Ruth asks me to wait over at their Customer Service area while she informs Jessica I am here to speak with her, "Give me a minute, please. She should be with you in a moment."

Ruth has to wrestle with her keys in order to unlock the security door that leads into the glass room, but she finally prevails. Ruth turns and pushes the door tightly closed, she then flips a knob on the upper door, turns around, and walks over to Jessica. Jessica looks up as Ruth approaches her. As they are speaking, they both look over in my direction. When both women turn back to look at each other, Jessica is shaking her head back and forth "No, no," and her hands go up, palms up, questioning Ruth. Ruth turns and glares my way.

Jessica leads the way, Ruth follows, as both women exit the glass room coming in my direction. Both women have a look of sternness on their faces as they march toward me. Cold, forbidding, and harsh looks are cast upon me as Jessica storms in on me, "Why are you here? What's your name again? I don't know you at all." I put my hands up like I am being arrested. "Sorry, I spoke with Rhonda over at Denny's. She talked with me about the Arctic tern tail feather earrings she bought here. Rhonda told me she knew you, to ask for Jessica. I am very sorry. Please, just let me leave now."

Jessica and Ruth both start laughing. "Please put your hands down. We're not police officers," the two ladies say to me in unison.

Jessica extends her hand. "Hi, I'm Jess."

Reluctantly, I take her snow white hand. "Hi, I'm Bob, Rhonda's buddy. Wow, you two had my heart pounding there for a moment. I thought we were going to need 9-1-1," I reply, while jokingly clutching at my chest.

Jessica excuses Ruth and turns slightly to her right. She throws me a seductive look over her left shoulder, "Are you following me? Let's go." As Jessica clears the counter area, I can see she is wearing a pair of black, leather cowboy boots. They come up the full length of the back of her calves, almost to her knees. The boots have big, black laces running up the entire front of her shins that lace them together.

The eyelets are robust and shiny gold, a petite square toe, medium heel, heavy sole, very nice boots indeed.

Jessica stops. She follows my eyes down, looks at her own boots then, seemingly frightened, snaps her head back up in my direction. "Do you like my boots?"

"Yes, I'm sorry, I didn't mean to stare. They are great."

She starts laughing at my apology. Jessica continues, "No, I'm glad you like them. My boyfriend hates them. He keeps telling me to return them or pawn them. try to get my money back so we can go out drinking. That's his big plan for our lives right now—go out drinking."

Jessica apologizes to me, "So sorry to carry on. Oh my, you are just that easy to talk with, Bob."

I need to interrupt her, so I ask, "Jessica, I am looking for an old friend. Her name is Andrea Altiery. Would you by any chance ever have heard of her?"

Jessica is shaking her head no, as she replies, "Andrea … Andrea Altiery. You know, that name does sound familiar to me for some reason. I just can't place it … No, I don't think I know of her, though, I am sorry."

Sullen and saddened, my head drops, my chin is resting on my chest. I decide to take a chance. Looking back to Jessica, I ask her, "Jessica, can we meet up later when you get out of work? I need to talk with you, but I also need to listen, so please meet up with me and tell me a story."

Jessica replies, "Sounds great, I love your energy. There's a glow about you that I like." Then she speaks the dreaded words that most guys hate, "You're so cute."

"Where do you want us to meet up?" I ask her.

Jessica replies, "Do you know Point Woronzof?"

I stare in disbelief. My face feels like it's turning white, embarrassment flows through me. "Yes I know the point pretty well, I was just there this morning, but I would be glad to go back and meet you there. What time?"

She replies, "2 p.m. Is that good for you?"

"2 p.m. sounds great. See you then, 2 p.m. at Point Woronzof," I confirm with her.

"It can seem like time stands still sometimes. This is especially true in a land with an endless horizon, a land like Alaska. You can't quantify its immensity. We try, but in the end it's the land that quantifies us, appraises us, evaluates us. I have flown into remote valleys in helicopters, jumping over mountain peaks adorned with rippling ridges, reflective tarns glittering back as we pass overhead, looking down like eager eagles, we will fear no evil in the valley today."

Jessica is right on time. She pulls into the Point Woronzof parking lot at exactly 2:15 p.m. She is driving a midnight blue Ford Mustang, and has a small pair of boxing gloves hanging off her rearview mirror—they are red, white, and blue. She has a cigarette hanging out of her mouth, and I can hear loud music. She is wearing a purple bandana wrapped around her auburn hair. It's sensual and sexy, alluring, yet down to earth.

Luckily the yellow Dodge van with hints of rust around every edge from this morning's public display of affection has departed. It's a yellow Dodge van loaded with drama, roaming the streets of Anchorage, looking to get plastered on cheap booze. Hopefully they won't create terror by committing vehicular homicide among the citizens. I shudder at the thought. Your telephone is ringing, it's 2:05 a.m., chills go down your spine as you sleepily reach out to answer the incoming telephone call. Is this finally the call every lover dreads?

It's an easy walk from the parking lot down onto the waterfront. Scattered driftwood, loosely strewn among the rocks, greet us. Jessica loves my accent, she keeps giggling while trying to understand my blubbering and stammering. I trip on some fishing line that's wrapped around a piece of driftwood. We both start laughing uncontrollably while I hop around on one foot. I find myself entangled in a spider web of lost dreams, frayed edges are chaffing at my tender ankles, boulders of contention have become my dance floor.

We walk south for a while, past the spot where the belugas cruised by our beach party back in 1982. Jessica and I stand still for a while, watching planes taking off and landing at Ted Stevens Airport. Behind us there's flocks of birds flying tight along the water's choppy surface. Migratory by nature and utilizing acclimatization for survival, millions fluttering, they swarm in waves into Alaska each year. Arctic terns fluttering in pulsing waves across the water's edge, blurring our vision, northward bound and restless.

Jessica explains to me that this is the best walk she has had since living in Alaska. "You don't seem like an outsider," she tells me.

"Yeah, I hear that a lot … it's in my blood. Alaska, that is, and Anchorage. I lived up here a long time ago, it just grabs you." Then I ask her the infamous, Alaskan question, "How long have you been living up here?"

Jessica responds with a proud look, "Seven years, too long maybe," her proud look rapidly dissolving into a sullen dismay.

We talk about Andrea Altiery and why I am still looking for her after all this time. "You must have really liked her," Jessica says while taking my arm. She snuggles into me as we walk. "You know, Jess, I'm conflicted, maybe it's the what ifs, that I am in love with. Just my romantic sentimentalism that's been misplaced all these years." Jessica squeezes my arm tighter, as we push into the increasing wind. The tail of her purple bandana is dancing teasingly across her back.

Suddenly we start to hear loud shouts. There are other people on the beach up ahead of us. It looks like they are throwing anything they can get their hands on, into the water. It also looks like one of them has a handgun. The man with the handgun starts acting aggressively. He swings his arms wildly, and begins aiming the handgun at the water. Jessica and myself both hear a loud "Bang ... Bang ... Bang." Yes, that would be a hand gun, and the aggressive guy with the handgun seems intent on killing something today. His buddies are jumping up and down, all of them are shrieking into the wind like a bunch of wild banshees.

Jessica begins to pull on my hand, she is leading me up through some boulders at the base of the bluff. As we stumble up through the bigger boulders attempting to go around the shooters and the throwers, Jessica stops and pulls me into her. She looks up into my face and says with a serious face, "I am hoping to avoid severe bodily harm, or even death, by a frenzied mob of thugs today. Bob, what did we get ourselves into out here?" I can't help but laugh, it's a nervous laugh, and Jessica responds to me with her own laugh.

After furiously clawing our way up a loose, sandy bluff, we get into the parking lot. Both of us are panting heavily and sweating profusely. Jessica removes her purple bandana and wipes her face with it. She hands it over to me. Her smell is intoxicating. The moisture from her skin has saturated the cloth with her scent. I wipe the bandana across my sweating forehead, slowly bringing it down across my wet face so I can catch her smell again. The scent of Jessica in the wild, mixed with ocean breeze, I start inhaling deeply.

All of a sudden I hear Jessica let out an ungodly wail. Her hands are covering her face, she is stomping her feet screaming, "No, no, he followed me ... that idiot followed me again, Bob." She is trembling, and pointing at her midnight blue Ford Mustang with the small pair of boxing gloves hanging off the rearview mirror—the gloves are red, white, and blue. The blue Mustang's antenna is now broken and dangling by a cord against the front quarter panel. The front quarter panel looks like someone kicked it in.

When we get over to the car, it's completely trashed. Both windshield wipers are broken right off, and have been placed on the hood of the car. Under the windshield wipers someone has left a note—the note simply reads, "WE ARE DONE, ME." There is a broken beer bottle that someone smashed on the roof of her car, beer has been poured all over the windshield, and rose petals have been tossed onto the beer. A sticky lava, of lost love, drizzled across her car's exterior, on full display for the public's viewing.

I can see Jessica is deeply bruised and battered, devoured by disdain, as she crumbles against the side of her car. Her body is heaving and quivering as she sobs, her heart is broken, crushed by the hate of another. I turn around looking up at the hillside of Anchorage, wondering if there is anyone looking down at us. I have an overwhelming feeling that a lot of us are trudging up there on Toilsome Hill Road, we are pursuing an evaporating dream, that dream seemingly being a love that's never going to be found for any of us.

# Chapter 9

# *Exotic Sea Gems*

Walking around the waterfront in Anchorage has always been one of my favorite ways to take in urban Alaska. Early in the spring of 1981 found me walking alone down on the coastal trail, I had walked down W.7th Ave to where it ends at the fence that encloses the railroad tracks. I jumped over the fence, and walked across the tracks to a little prominent point of land that juts out into Cook Inlet—it's a great vantage point. There's a lot of driftwood to sit on, and it's a great place to just listen and watch.

Walking south along the trail, when I get to where Stolt Lane meets S Street, I decide to cut up through a little thicket of woods that separate the trail and railroad tracks. I will walk across the railroad tracks again and jump over the enclosure fence. Then I can walk Stolt Lane into S Street, over to W.11th Avenue. Walk P Street to W.10th Avenue. This will get me over onto the Delaney Park Strip. It should be a cake walk, a stroll through the park on a sunny day.

When I get into the middle of the thicket it gets very muddy and swampy. My boots become muddy and slippery, which causes me to slip on the fence. As I clamor to grab hold of the fence, my inner forearm gets scraped harshly on a protruding bolt. My soft skin burning and stinging, an intense stabbing pain jolts up my arm. I'm jumping up and down shaking my arm, *if only I had kept my denim jacket sleeve buttoned, see you had to not button the sleeve, it would have protected you if it had been buttoned, it might not have pulled back and exposed your skin, but no, you had to leave it unbuttoned.*

As my dance of pain diminishes, I start laughing at myself, looking around. I am glad to be alone, but also realizing that if anybody can see me right now I must look insane. I stumble over to Stolt Lane and continue on my way, pressing the sleeve of my jacket into the cut to stop the seeping blood. The pain continues to linger, my arm is throbbing.

Two older gentlemen, both walking menacing looking dogs, leashed on heavy chains along W.11th Ave, cause me to step out into the street to walk by them. Both dogs are glaring at me, their mouths hanging open, tongues drooling, spiked collars glistening. I can hear the tinkling of the dog tags that are hanging from thick leather collars. As they strut by me, they are snarling contempt under their dog breaths. Both guys tip their hats.

Pleased and delighted, I have finally arrived at P Street and W.10th Avenue. I stop and look out across almost a mile of green park that is spread out before me. Green grass, along with trees and flowering shrubs push off into the distance toward snow laden mountain peaks. There's a lot of people in the park right now. I think I'll walk right up the middle of the grass through the crowd. I need to find something to drink, and maybe sit down for a while. Maybe I can wash my cut with some water. The blood has soaked through my jacket sleeve, and it's leaving a huge red stain on the material.

After walking for about a hundred yards, I come to a small garden with some benches in the middle of the lawn. There are dogs running around being chased by laughing children. There's a red balloon that's freely floating up into the sky. I can see a woman kneeling next to a small boy. The boy is rubbing his eyes and the woman seems to be consoling him. They both look up and wave goodbye to the balloon as it floats away. The balloon seems to be drifting aimlessly higher, unaware that its absence causes anguish.

I see a slouching lady with a small vendor's cart—she is selling water, soda, juice, and snacks. I join the small line that's waiting, when two guys walk over to me asking, "Hey, buddy, we need some money. Can you help us out?" They are both standing here glaring at me, their black-and-white baseball caps are pulled down over their eyes. The other people in the slouching lady's line look my way, looks of caution and concern wash across all of their faces.

I respond, "I was hoping you guys could lend me some cash, maybe take me out on a date, and introduce me to your mothers."

Everyone starts laughing, including the two imposing guys with black-and-white baseball caps. An older guy in line turns around and jokes, "You can meet my mother and you can take my wife at the same time."

Everyone is laughing again. I take a five dollar bill out of my back pocket and give it to one of the guys, "Here, you can share this, but that's it, no more, ok?"

Both of the guys thank me, they shake my hand and welcome me to Alaska, "We really hope you find what you are looking for out here, my friend."

As I pay for my water, the slouching lady who owns the cart tells me she liked the way I handled the two would-be ruffians. "I like your sense of humor, but I really love your accent," she responds, while grinning sheepishly up into my face.

I reply, "Thank you very much, and I love your accent also. Please be safe out here today."

"Always," she responds.

As soon as I turn around, I hear a voice yelling, "Hey, soldier boy, over here, soldier boy." I freeze—it's the smiling girl with the cowboy hat I met a few days back. We both wave at once, both of us smiling profusely in each other's directions. She is yelling, "Come here, come over here," so I walk in her direction, happy to see she is actually sitting on a bench today, to keep us off the damp grass.

I eagerly walk over to her, grinning, "Hey, it's good to see you again. I'm glad you called out to me."

"I'm glad you actually heard me and came over. Sit down, please," she replies. Quickly and gently, with the flat of her hand, she touches the empty spot on the bench next to her. Her jewelry is glistening in the sun, her lightly tanned skin is absorbing the gold's hue blending it into a potpourri of passionate elegance. It's beckoning to the wild within me; some distant memory seems to be gripping my soul.

I tease her as I begin to sit, "So how goes it? Can the smiling lady tell me a story today?"

She gladly obliges me. Her voice, steady cadence, starts expounding on her future. "There's my house right over there," she is pointing over in the direction of W. 10th Avenue. My eyes follow her strong forearm, with short but neatly manicured fingers, they are pointing over to our right. We both glance that way.

I am nodding, "I like your neighborhood. Please continue."

"I want to go to school for gemology and jewelry design, become skilled in the act of creating fine jewelry. I want to open a jewelry shop in downtown Anchorage. In my jewelry shop, I want to have an inspiring space named Exotic Gems of the Sea. This inspiring space will become my masterpiece of creation, where I can feel safe to be free and create, surrounded by ocean blue walls."

"That's an intriguing vision, soothing to the senses. Please continue," I encourage her. I am smiling intently into her deep, dark, brown eyes. Her eyes capture my soul, and then for a moment, I feel frightened.

To have a beautiful woman open up like this to me is a new experience, a lady with a plan that can paint a vision for her future. She has my attention, she gets my blood moving. I reach over and clasp her hand. She squeezes my fingers as she folds our hands together into her stomach, allowing and inviting me to feel the warmth of her core's essence.

The warm lady continues, "I really want to have children, but with the right man. That's my fear, right? What happens if we have kids, and then he leaves me alone with children to fend for ourselves?"

"Life has no guarantees, that's the uncertainty, that's what causes our hesitations, I can understand that fear," I reply to her.

Suddenly, and without any warning, a feisty black dog, with a stick in his mouth, comes crashing over to us. He starts jumping up onto our knees, he is shaking his head back and forth with the stick, he seems to be trying very hard to get our attention.

There's a grumpy looking guy, he is quickly walking toward us, yelling, "Snoopy, come here, Snoopy, get down."

Snoopy turns his head, he has thick, black, wiry fur, with a white patch running down his chest. With his paws resting on the smiling lady's feet, he looks right into her face. Snoopy starts shaking his head back and forth again.

The big stick is protruding out of each side of his mouth, his ears stiffen when he hears his name again, "Snoopy come ... Snoopy," the owner calls.

Snoopy jumps for joy at his name, the owner looks over at me and growls, "What are you looking at, buddy? Take a picture." Suddenly Snoopy drops the stick from out of his mouth and starts chasing another dog.

There's a lady with the dog, and she starts screaming, "Candy ... Candy, come back here, honey." Snoopy wants some Candy today, like we all want candy, it keeps life sweet.

I look over at Snoopy's grumpy owner, "To answer your question, sir, I am looking at you, I am looking at someone who can't control his dog," I snarl in his direction.

Grumpy guy puts his hands up, muttering under his breath as he is walking away, "Have a good one, buddy. Snoopy, let's roll, come on."

The smiling lady in the cowboy hat is standing up to leave, explaining to me that she needs to go get ready for work. She also tells me, "I hope we get to speak again, maybe have lunch sometime." We shake hands while smiling into each other's eyes. I am nodding yes, yes to all of it.

I don't want to let her hand go, not yet, so I linger with my gentle grasp. We both let our fingers slide away from each other slowly, we keep our hands extended out toward each other as we walk away. Longingly looking over our shoulders, we look back into each other's eyes. It seems like I am moving in slow motion, as I watch her gracefully glide away from me.

Today I am going to use my car and drive over to 335 Boniface Parkway and grab a few shots of whiskey at Carpentiers Lounge. Back in 1981, Andrea Altiery had told me she was meeting a guy in their parking lot to do a photo shoot for $300.

"Bob, an hour's work for $300," is how Andrea had explained it to me.

Quick, easy, and fun is how the customer had explained it to Andrea. Carpentiers Lounge is where I had my first beer in Alaska. It is close to two nearby military bases, and Arctic Valley. Arctic Valley is a vast wilderness, right in Anchorage's backyard.

Immediately upon stepping into the lounge, I am met with loud music coming from the juke box, the band The Go Gos are singing, "We know you can dance to the beat, we got the beat, jumpin' and get down, we got the beat." There's an extremely beautiful and curvaceous young woman writhing to the beat alone, in the middle of the floor. I step over to the bar as I continue watching her dance. My hand starts tapping to the beat on the bar top. I order whiskey on the rocks—let's go, take it nice and slow in here today.

As the song dies down, the curvaceous young woman sensually struts over toward me. She is smiling as she walks by me. Both of our heads turn as we follow each other's gazes. She stops, and behind her on the wall I can see a poster of a blonde haired girl. The blonde haired girl is sitting in a big cocktail glass. She is wearing a red bra, red shoes, red undies with an angel's face, smiling. Carpentiers Lounge is welcoming me home again.

The curvaceous young woman motions for me to come over to her. I grab my drink and walk to her. Her face is smooth and symmetrical. Her shaggy black hair is sweeping over her strong neck. She is wearing a silver necklace that has a small whale's tooth braided into the chain. It's intricate and delicate. Her smile is infectious and irresistible, it's like being caught in a fishing net that is woven from grasses and other fibrous plant material. I am unable to struggle free, its softness grabs onto me and pulls me toward her.

Too attractive, and tempting to be resisted, I reach my hand out. She firmly takes my hand. "Hi, I'm Michelle, but you can call me Shelly,"

"Hi, I'm Bob. Just call me Bob."

Michelle smiles and replies, "Hi, Bob, nice to meet you. Can we get out of here now?"

My eyes open wide, my throat freezes and goes dry, I start choking because this never ends good for me, but she's a temptress, and I can't resist her. I motion to the bartender and order another round for both of us. I ask him to close my tab out, let me pay the check, and leave with Michelle.

"I have some great bud we can smoke," Michelle whispers into my ear. She starts rubbing my shoulders as she walks up behind me. I feel her suddenly grab around my waist, and she starts rubbing her head firmly into my back. I like the feel of this. Michelle walks around to my left side, she traces her right fingers across my left shoulder sensually, she shakes her hair while turning to face me.

"We outta here, Bob, I've been dancing alone for too long in here today."

My head is nodding yes. I reply, "Sure, let's do it. My car is right outside. Let's go."

There's a raw edge about Michelle, her beauty is complex and layered. It's like peeling a precious and tender fruit that oozes its sticky juices all over your hands, and your fingers instinctively go to your lips, tasting her sugary liquid of love. You inhale the fragrance of her aroma, of that lingering scent, deeply and fully into the core of your soul. Michelle is that tantalizing, and mesmerizing.

Michelle is from Savoonga. Savoonga is on St. Lawrence island. "It's raw and kind of savage out there sometimes," she tells me, shaking her head. "My land is beautiful, it's raw Alaska, I think you would like to visit my village, maybe someday, huh?"

I reply, "Sounds enchanting, please tell me more. Michelle, I love your accent, it's smooth and sensual, keep talking, please."

Michelle smiles and continues. "Sometimes I can feel complete emptiness out there," a look of despair, clouds her face. She removes a pack of cigarettes from her sweater pocket. As she lights the cigarette, she begins to lower the passenger's side window, "Sometimes I just hate myself out there."

Michelle continues, "I'm on a journey to heal my inner void."

I look over at her and respond, "Your inner void …?"

Michelle lowers her head, nodding yes, "It's terribly painful, and it gives me a feeling of desolation. It's like I have this gaping inner hole inside me."

I respond, "Wow Michelle, please if I can help you on this journey in any way, here's my ear, please continue."

I reach over and take her left hand. Her hands are rough like sand paper, gritty, she pulls her hands away and explains it's from pulling fishing nets back home in her village. Seemingly embarrassed, she folds her hands onto her lap.

Michelle continues to expound and convey with a broken voice, "As the feelings intensify, so do my desires to seek relief, self-medicate. So I reach for another cigarette, the fridge, the bottle, the remote control."

Suddenly she grabs onto my right arm, spins toward me, and exclaims, "Or my next sexual conquest," while smiling at me in a provocative, teasing way. Then, with a serious look, Michelle stares into my eyes, "Do you want me to pump your brains out today?" Now she has my attention. I glance sideways at her and push down hard on the gas pedal.

We wait until we arrive in the hotel room before we smoke any bud—no need to take the risk while driving—mix two shots of whiskey with a few tokes of good bud—now that's really impaired. As soon as we step into the hotel room and the door closes, Michelle grabs me and kisses me, she pushes me back onto the bed, jumps up onto me while straddling my chest.

She is staring down at me, her nostrils are flaring in a seductive way, "You think you can handle me? You think you can take me?" Michelle breaks into a hysterical laugh as she rolls off my chest and back down onto my bed. She rolls up and leans her chin onto her left palm, she flips her hair casually off her shoulder.

"Mind if I take a shower while you roll us a joint to smoke, okay, is that sweet for you, my friend Bob?" she asks me.

I reply "Absolutely, yes, the shower is yours for the next twenty minutes, and your time starts … now." I snap my hand as I motion for her to get up and go. I am pointing her toward the bathroom door.

Michelle jumps up running, and looks back, smiling at me, "Time me," she yells, while slamming the bathroom door behind her.

I start thinking about a song done by The Beatles, *It's Only Love*. in the song they are singing to a woman named

Michelle, "I need to make you see, oh, what you mean to me, my Michelle." I can imagine laying my head on Michelle's damp chest, when she gets out of the shower, *I can hear your heart beat now, Michelle, the rhythm of it is drumming in my ear.*

The bathroom door opens, and Michelle comes walking out with a towel wrapped around her upper body. Her lower body is naked. Her soaking, wet hair, is hanging around her graceful neck. She is crying. Sobbing, she throws her heaving body onto my bed. With her face down, she starts hammer fisting the bed into submission. She is wailing loudly. "My body is so ugly ... you're going to hate me, I hate me, why would you like me, I hate me, I hate me," her fists continue to beat the bed into submission.

Good for you, Michelle, you go girl, beat them, bust them, break them down.

I jump over onto the bed, and gently straddle her left leg, lightly rubbing down onto her. I move up onto the curves of her buttocks. I reach out and pull on the towel that's covering her back to undo it. When I pull it back away from her, I am aghast, I am filled with shock at what I am seeing, appalled into silence. Michelle looks back at me, "See, it's ugly, right? Am I right?" I've never seen so many burns and scars on a human being in my life.

Her back looks like someone took a fillet knife and just started hacking and slashing, I collapse and start crying with her. My face falls into the small of her back, she reaches back and grabs onto my hair as we both cry. My eyes are looking along the curves of her buttocks and I know it's savage, yet sensual. I finally reach over and grab the joint of bud I rolled. We light it up and just smoke in silence. Michelle keeps lying on her stomach with my head resting on her lower back. Dazed and glazed, I stare up at the ceiling fan whirring in slow motion above our heads.

I can feel my waning desires, withering, among a frozen wilderness. My only desire right now is to reach out and heal Michelle. My gift for her would be to rub her scars away with rose petal oils and lavender, mixed into an aloe vera gel. We will light a sweet incense, and drink a bitter tea together. Our hands tightly clasped, we will smile together, until all her mental scars fade into oblivion.

Michelle tells me she is game for taking a ride out to Point Woronzof. "We can relax out there, Michelle. Take it slow and enjoy our time together."

She responds, "I need that, Bob, thanks, you are great. You don't just listen to me, you can actually feel me, it seems," her head is nodding. We both smile profusely at each other.

"Let's rock, let's go," I give her my hand, and she eagerly accepts it, without pulling away.

As we pull into the Point Woronzof parking lot, I can see five other cars parked. A few of the cars have small groups of people standing around outside talking, taking pictures, and drinking beer. Michelle gets excited and starts pointing toward one of the cars, "Go over there, I know those people, they are my people."

As I am pulling in next to the car Michelle directed me to, she jumps out yelling, and the five women that are standing next to the car all turn around at once. They start jumping up and down yelling, "No way, Shelly … it's Shelly." As they bounce up and down, the excitement is contagious. For me, the excitement is that I am alone with six women at Point Woronzof, standing here with six Alaskan women in the shadows of Susitna—can it get any better?

A girl named Beverly, from Ambler, starts talking to us about her old teacher, and basketball coach. She is telling us she has a crush on him, Beverly says, "His name is Nick Jans. He is a great man. I want to marry him someday." All the other women start laughing at her, telling her to dream on. I just look at her and think to myself, *sounds like a girl with a plan to me, dream on, Bev*. The cognac comes out, and we all start swigging as the wind picks up, while brooding Beverly stays silent in the background.

We have a nice, warm, cognac glow going when the five women tell us they are leaving. They ask us if we would be able to meet them down on W.4th Ave at the Gaslight Lounge in about two hours. Michelle wants us to meet up with them, and I am open, so we agree. "Sure, ok, in two hours we will be there," I tell the women. They all jump over to shake my hand and hug me. Each one tells me I don't remind them of an outsider. "You're not like the other outsiders. We like your spirit." I'm glad to hear this, it makes my spirit soar above the inlet's white capped tides, like a fluttering kite on a windy day, clouds drifting overhead accompanying me as I soar.

As the five women pull out of the parking lot, we wave goodbye. "Let's get out of this wind," Shelly says. Her body is shaking inside her sweater, she is pulling the collar tight around her neck. We jump into the red Pontiac Grand Am. It has less than four thousand miles on its engine. The interior of the car is spotless, the windows are still pristine, which is a rarity in the rough road state of Alaska, with its rutted grooves, seismic cracks, and tectonic troughs waiting to swallow the unsuspecting.

Michelle looks over at me from her passenger side seat, "Hey, Bob, will you let me drive this baby?"

"No I can't, Michelle. You're not on my insurance."

She glares at me with a menacing grimace. "What did you just say to me? What did you just say? You're not going to let me drive the car, after you saw me naked? I promise I'll pump your brains out, just let me drive." Michelle puts her feet up onto my dashboard, while leaning back into her seat gingerly. She is glancing sideways out her side window.

She keeps talking, "What, you don't like me? You think I'm going to smash this thing up, right?"

I turn in my seat to face her, "Listen, Michelle, please back down, that's not happening, not today, probably not tomorrow. You can't drive."

Michelle starts shrieking, she turns her feet toward me and starts kicking on me like a crazed moose—hard kicks, wallops that hurt. I'm talking heavy blows that have the intent to do damage, severe bodily harm.

Michelle spins and turns the fury of her shod feet against my windshield. The assault continues against the innocent glass. Every kick causes tiny spider webs of cracks to flash across the windshield. She jumps over and rips the rearview mirror off the windshield, and frantically starts swinging it at me. She slams me in my mouth with the mirror, she begins snarling venom, and starts spitting into my hair.

I'm screaming "Calm down ... calm down."

She is screaming, "You just think I'm a stupid girl ... a stupid girl, right?"

Michelle opens up my passenger's side door, she continues her verbal assault as she exits my vehicle. I am being barraged with unsolicited advice from a crazed woman. Michelle continues to spit all over my dashboard as she exits my vehicle.

She looks back at me, with one last menacing snarl, "You're so selfish, I hate you," she slams my door shut, BANG.

I can see Mount Susitna in the background, across Cook Inlet, she is offering me her noble presence. I rest my forehead into my right hand, as I look off to my left. *Katmai beckons to the carnivore within me. Kenai has yet to be resurrected from her ashes. Bold waves splash at the foot of the bluffs I am sitting on, and sometimes the earth quakes here, sending showers of shimmering blue glacial water, infusing me into its roiling waves.*

# Chapter 10

# *Andrea Alaskan Angel*

What calls us back to our past? The superstitions that guided us in our youth, maybe it's a glimmer of hope for our future, I don't know. You think you're stepping into God's house but find yourself strolling through the stem of the devil's den, finding the journey is fear-based and panic-fed. You find yourself being sieged upon by wolves that come to you clothed in lamb skins, presenting purity tests that they themselves can't pass. They are eager to pounce in spiritual superiority, spiritual bullies living in glass houses, always throwing stones your way

It's a bleak, blustery Saturday morning, and as I am driving toward Arctic Valley, I randomly pull over into the parking lot of a small church. I am not really sure why I am here, but I follow my gut. As I pull into their parking lot, they have a banner hanging up that welcomes you to their Sabbath school, 9:30 a.m.–10:15 a.m. All Welcome, the sign reads. I could use a warm welcome this morning, maybe even coupled with a smile. As I step into their front foyer, I am met with a lot of eager handshakes, and salutations of happy Sabbath, glad to meet you, hope you can stay for our potluck lunch after the service today.

I get directed toward a set of open doors, and I step into a dimly lit auditorium. I can see that all the women have hats on, all the hats are adorned with flowers, pins, and brooches, and loud amens are ringing out in the background. The man standing up front, speaking on the stage, is informing everyone we are living in the very last moments of earth's history. Today is the day, the man shouts. He gets cheered with loud shouts of "Amen, brother," accompanied by vigorous, raucous clapping that is disturbingly harsh to my ears.

The standing man continues to speak, "The fire that's burning up in Big Lake right this moment, that fire is going to swoop down into this valley, the winds are going to drive it up that hillside, where it's gonna burn all those people looking down on us. Can I get an Amen to that?" Loud shouts begin to ring out, "Amen, brother," but this time the congregation is standing up to clap for his words—an array of adorned hats vigorously nodding their approval.

At this point, I am becoming a little concerned, because the other day I went to look at a house up on the hillside, on Sultana Drive. I had met with a realtor named Tom. Tom is from Jack White Realty Company, he did the showing for me. Maybe it would be best for me to keep this news to myself, amid this hostile, raucous crowd of revelry.

Suddenly I am not feeling welcomed at all. My body stiffens as I realize I need to vacate the premises, and as quickly as possible. As I begin to stand so I can leave, I can hear the talking man continue to expound. "Brothers and sisters, I offer you one last convincing piece of evidence that the end is not just near, but it's here," amid shouts of "Amen, brother, tell us like it is." Dumbfounded at the words I hear next, I stop and turn to face him while he is speaking.

"My brothers and my sisters, it's a solemn morning. This past week, I went fishing over at Ship Creek." He stares into the crowd, he is glaring at us with a dazed look of confusion on his face. He lowers his microphone down below his waist and bows his head. When he looks up, he explains, "They have instituted In-and-Out Fees at Ship Creek, can you believe this, In-and-Out Fees at Ship Creek. If you leave and return, you have to repay the fee." The congregation jumps up again amid another round of shouts, "Amen, brother, tell us like it is." I quickly walk up the dimly lit aisle so I can exit the auditorium. I am thinking, *oh fervent disciples of deception, let us loudly clap.*

A gentle, smiling woman standing next to the front door asks me why I am leaving so soon. I gingerly take her hand to shake it, and I explain to her, "Listen, if the world is about to end like I just heard in your auditorium, I am going out to enjoy it while I still have a chance." I give her a big smile.

She responds to me with a withering look of dismay.

While I am walking out the door, I am thinking, *I better not go fishing over at Ship Creek, the devil may try to shake me down for a toll to cross the foot bridge.*

Once I get out on the Glenn Highway, the traffic is light. I come driving up on a small bull moose that's running along the right shoulder. He is wildly looking to cross the road, his eyes are bulging. I watch the young bull moose in my rearview mirror as he bolts across the highway toward Ship Creek and the Cottonwood Park area. I turn off the highway at Fort Richardson. As I begin the lazy drive through the Moose Run Golf Course area to start the ascent up into Arctic Valley, my mind begins to drift into a very vivid daydream.

In this daydream, Andrea and I are riding on a vintage French carousel. Draped in fancy canopies, it spins in a room full of mirrors. There's a glass staircase that brings you into an upper observation room. From this observation room, you can see the beginning, to the end, of all eternity. We walk up the stairs and find two horses sitting in the middle of the room, both of them waiting for their riders. Both horses are adorned with Arctic bell strings buckled around their girths. A slight breeze causes the Arctic bell strings to start ringing as Andrea and myself approach our horses.

Andrea is riding a pale horse, and her horse's name is Despair. I am riding on a white horse, and my horse's name is Conquest. Both the horses are adept at mountain travel and both are muscular and lean, their faces forever frozen in fierce grimaces.

As we slowly whir around in mesmerizing circles, we are filled with delight, and charmed, as we pass by a slender, magical, metallic chute. This chute contains silver and gold rings that slide down into a grooved finger notch. As we pass by the finger notch, on the end of the chute, the goal is for us to reach out with a single finger, trying to grab onto a ring. If you miss and don't grab onto a ring, or if you grab onto a silver ring, there's no next time for you to enjoy your ride. You must promptly exit from the grounds, never being allowed to return.

If you are lucky enough to grab onto a gold ring, this brings you the reward, and you avoid the punishment of banishment. You continue to ride, against soft breezes that caress your face, and vibrant, pipe organ music—melancholic notes ringing in the background, they massage our aching hearts.

We continue to smile. Andrea has her head leaning back. She is letting her long, brown, auburn hair flow with the breeze. As we pass by the chute, I grab onto a gold ring, and with gushing displays of affection toward Andrea, I hoist the gold ring above my head for her to behold.

Andrea lets her arm poetically swing out with a graceful, elongated expression, and her hand gracefully reaches for her ring. She pulls the ring out of the chute and holds it above her head in triumph. Excitedly, she looks up at the color of her ring, but suddenly her face melts into a dismal look of despair.

She has grabbed the last, feeble and unimpressive, pale pearl ring, known to be in existence. Her horse Despair is quick to react—he rears up on his muscular hind legs. His auburn colored mane is twisting wildly in the wind, his angry eyes flash fire, and there is smoke billowing out of his nostrils, which is aromatic like mountain cedar.

With a sharp thud, our horses jump off the carousel and start running down the glass staircase. Andrea turns in her saddle to look back toward me. Overcome with desperation, she starts pleading for me to help her. I can hear Andrea yelling for me, "Bob, I need you to look into my eyes, look into my eyes."

When I look into Andrea's eyes, I instantly become placed under a spell—one of her eyes is deep blue, the other eye is sparkling green. With a desperate lunge, I reach out for Andrea, but her horse Despair is salaciously sweeping her away.

Shockingly, and without any warning, everything goes dark, the lights get turned off, the music has stopped now, and the carousel slowly spins to a wobbling standstill. My shaky and unstable legs buckle under me as I step off my horse. My hand grabs firmly onto the reins, as Conquest stumbles on the stairs.

Suddenly, I find myself alone and, in the dark, I stumble the rest of the way down the glass staircase while trying to locate Andrea. As I walk through all the horses on the carousel, all the horses' eyes are looking at me, with frozen looks of fear. All of their nostrils are flaring, wide and red. I bend down, so I can look through the horses twisted legs—each horse, with adorned hooves lifted, frozen in its own step of time, their faces are locked in grimaces of fear.

As the road turns from pavement to gravel, I get jolted back into familiar surroundings. I love Arctic Valley road; I have walked, skied, and driven on it many times. There's a lot of mystery in these mountains, snowlines creeping down mountainsides, the valley is wild and deep. It calls to the wild within me. Remote, deep tarns, surrounded by jagged peaks. Temptation Peak towers like a lone sentinel whose job it is to stand and keep watch over the lonely valley, which is in its shadows.

I indulge into my next daydream—Andrea Altiery and I are sitting on the top of Temptation Peak. We are overlooking the valley below, our eyes are following a delicate ridgeline that divides the valley, off into the horizon. We are looking down at a golden carpet of tundra, speckled with flocks of ptarmigan that are feeding on fermenting blueberry bushes. The bushes are heavy, with fat fruits. Wild rose bushes, whose fading flowers seem to frown and wilt in the early morning frost, carry the aroma of autumn, both pungent and raw.

Andrea reaches out for my hand. Her soft skin is glowing warm to my touch, we lean our heads into each other's shoulders as we hug. We both look up at the same time. Our lips meet, the kiss is passionate, her tongue teases me into submission, the submission is deep. Andrea jumps up and kneels over me, she pushes my head back with both hands, Andrea is looking directly into my eyes, one of her eyes is twinkling blue, the other eye is sparkling green—both wishful whirlpools of swirling lust.

I can hear her gentle voice, persuasive in its tones, "I need you to be with me through all this, Bob, I need you to take me into your arms. I need you to hold me tight." Andrea is smiling, her head is slightly bouncing as she nods approvingly toward me.

I respond, "Come into my arms, let me gently hold you and smell your hair." We embrace, her intoxicating touch is rousing, stirring.

I hear Andrea's voice, "I need you to hold me tight, Bob, please, just hold me tight, don't ever let me go. Hold me into eternity."

Andrea's body starts quivering, she seems fraught and overcome with fear, like something undesirable is about to happen to her. All of a sudden I become startled and frightened, thinking I must have seen a ghost. Andrea is descending down into the valley below me, she is disappearing into the clouds. She is riding a pale, winged horse, wings folding, then they disappear. I am looking intently down into the valley, watching as she goes.

Suddenly, two women dressed in purple and silver gowns are standing next to me. In unison they ask me, "Why do you stand here looking down into the valley?" Their hands are spread out in an encompassing, sweeping motion toward the valley below. Looks of curious inquiry are frozen on their faces.

My gaze follows the two women as they point below me into the lonely valley below, when suddenly I realize my heart is burning like a hot furnace within me. When I turn around, the two women are gone, but I am left with a wild urge to flee. Panic sets in, sudden, uncontrollable fear and anxiety over take me. I shiver in anguish, I become frightened and excited at the same time. Fear is pulsing through the valley in torrential waves, and it's creeping in to grab me, like a shadow from my past.

# *Andrea Altiery Human Being*

I never did find Andrea Altiery on that trip, or even locate anyone that could, or would talk with me about her. I never thought of going to the APD or AST, and the internet was not a part of my life in 1996.

When you find out that someone you care about is killed by a greedy, lustful, savage beast, your mind becomes tormented with graphic images, both raw and savage, of what may have happened. But I am comforted knowing that Andrea was a fighter, she was tenacious like a Kenai wolverine, her ripping fingers tearing and her strong, slapping hands, striking back.

Andrea Altiery was a beautiful human being with hopes and dreams. Andrea was constantly being amazed by the overall variety and beauty of Alaska. Her life was selfishly crushed and snatched away from her by a thief in the darkness of night. He was a vicious vandal causing her destruction. Andrea never had a chance to have a family and to give birth to her daughter Andromeda. With these writing's I am attempting to allow Andrea Altiery to live in the collective dreams of the planet.

Life is a process for all of us, our dreams are a process, and that process may never end.

*"... There was a beautiful girl standing next to me, but now she is gone. Suddenly I find myself standing in the valley of temptation again, Andrea's voice is calling out to me from below. I can see a smiling woman, she is standing in a shabby, chic, sunroom, and she is gifted in the art of creating fine jewelry..."*